FATAL AFFAIR

This one is for Charlotte French

FATAL AFFAIR

ONE

Well, my landlady had warned me.

"Oh, Miss Carr!" she had said. Disapproval had seemed to lengthen her already long Irish upper lip. "You couldn't know, being brand-new to London, but nice young women don't go wandering around Soho alone at night."

It was not yet really night. The gray twilight of a warm but overcast September day lingered in this ancient street sloping upward from bustling Piccadilly Circus. And yet even this early I could see what Mrs. Ryan had meant.

To come to this neighborhood I had worn the plainest clothes I had brought with me from New York—a plaid cotton skirt, a white cotton shirt, and an old suede jacket. I had looped my reddish-brown hair behind my ears. I wore no cosmetics, not even the liquid makeup with which I often cover the line of freckles across the bridge of my nose. Nevertheless, as I moved up the sidewalk, past the strip joints and porno shops and establishments offering everything from imported tea to fish and chips, I was aware of the scrutiny of male pedestrians. I was sure that they must be giving the same look of cold assessment to other women who walked, singly or in pairs, along this street, women of all ages from late teens to middle age, many of them in boots and tight miniskirts, some giggling and provocative-eyed, others with set, even grim, expressions.

About fifty feet ahead of me a long limousine angled to the curb. A uniformed chauffeur got out and opened the car's rear door. Two gray-haired couples in evening clothes emerged, crossed the sidewalk, and were bowed by a doorman into a restaurant.

"No, I don't think it's like your Times Square," Mrs. Ryan had said in answer to my question. "Soho's not all hoors and dirty-book stores. Nobs go there, too. Some of the poshest restaurants in London are there, and some of the most expensive grocers."

I went on past the "posh" restaurant. In its plate-glass window a row of loosely woven beige curtains obscured the lower half of the interior but not the elaborate crystal chandeliers hanging from the ceiling. Next to the restaurant stood a shop with a sign above its doorway, SM BOOK STORE, although its display windows held neither books nor anything else. A quick glance through its open doors into a long, glaringly lighted room showed me men standing in the aisles between the book-piled counters, each man alone, each with his gaze fixed on the open book in his hand. I had a sudden sense of the loneliness of those solitary men, and I felt not just revulsion but a twinge of sympathy.

And then everything else was driven from my mind,

because for one awful moment I thought I was looking at a photograph of Betsy.

It was in the window of an establishment next to the bookshop, a narrow-fronted place with the words "Thirty-two Club" on a sign above its door. Its display windows held photographs of several young women, but the one that riveted my attention was a large blowup of a blond girl, naked except for high-heeled shoes and a narrow drape, one end of which she clutched under her chin. But after I had stood for a second or two, overwhelmed by sorrowful guilt, I realized that the girl was not Betsy. True, this woman's face was somewhat similar, oval and with small, even features, but she was several years past my little sister's age, eighteen, and about ten pounds heavier.

Shaken, I moved on. Undoubtedly the strip joint's name referred to its address. Even though I'd heard that to Americans London's system of street numbering seemed erratic, I could hope that I was nearing the address I sought, 62 Malta Street.

A blare of sound as a basement doorway up ahead opened. A group of teenage boys and girls surged up onto the sidewalk and then turned left toward Piccadilly Circus. At least to my ear, educated by those English-made sagas on public television, their accents sounded working-class. So here was another element that, along with the rich restaurantgoers and the patrons of kinky bookstores, was attracted to this strange neighborhood.

And then I became aware of the music rising from the cellar from which the teenagers had emerged. Johnny Cash's recorded voice singing "I'll Walk the Line." American music. Rhythm-and-blues music.

Missouri music.

For a moment I was back in Carrsville, that town named for my great-great-grandfather, a sleepy little town that, tucked into the southeastern corner of Missouri, was more southern than middle western. The hot summer nights were filled with the song of mockingbirds. Cotton grew in fields surrounding the town. There was even a Confederate soldier leaning on his rifle in the town square, gloved marble hands crossed on the gun's stock, marble gaze remembering men who had died young more than a century ago.

No restaurants in Carrsville with patrons who wore evening dress. No kinky bookshops. And no "hoors," at least not any that Betsy and I had heard about.

How I wished that we had never left that town. If we had not, by now Betsy might be engaged or even married to one of the many boys who had swarmed around her ever since she was twelve. At least she would not be lost to me somewhere in this foreign city, if indeed she was still in this city and not somewhere else, perhaps a place I had never heard of.

It was my fault we had left Carrsville late in the previous spring. Oh, not that Betsy had not been eager to leave. But she was still a few days short of her eighteenth birthday. I was eight years older, surely old enough to have realized what could happen to small-town girls in headlong pursuit of what might turn out to be a chimera. . . .

I crossed a street, forgetting until a squeal of brakes reminded me that I should have looked to my right rather than my left. I passed two more doorways. Then there it was, the Café Ambroscadero.

Impossible to tell from the outside whether this was one of Soho's more fashionable restaurants. True, there

4

was a doorman, but scarcely an impressive one. He was twenty at most, and his uniform, designed for a much larger man, made him look younger still. He appeared to be an Indian, or perhaps a Pakistani. But then, even though I'd been in London only a few hours, I already had formed the impression that most of the low-paying jobs were held by Indians or other Asiatics.

I approached him. He gave me a startled look from dark, liquid eyes and then remembered to salute,

"Do you know where I could find Mr. Bracely?"

I could tell he had understood me. And yet he said, in a wary voice, "Pardon, miss?"

"Mr. Colin Bracely. He's the owner of this restaurant, or at least one of the owners, isn't he?"

Deepening unease in the dark young face. It must be that he was afraid of Colin. But that wasn't surprising. Even Colin's mother had said that sometimes she was afraid of him.

"I'm his cousin," I said, "from America."

Some of the worry left his face. Then, as a taxicab stopped at the curb, he seemed to come to a decision. Perhaps my claim of relationship to his boss had reassured him. Perhaps my plain clothes, or my freckles, inspired trust. Anyway, he said, "Go up those stairs over there." Then he turned to open the cab door for a young man in gray slacks and a new but cheap-looking blazer and a girl in a green polyester pantsuit. I turned toward an open doorway near the café's entrance.

Dim light from above shone on the narrow stairs. When I reached the landing I turned to my right toward the only visible door. Varnish, so newly applied that the smell lingered, covered the walls. On the floor was a dark red carpet that looked as if it would be harsh to the touch. It was like the clothing of that young couple, new but cheap-looking. If this building could be taken as evidence, my cousin was not yet the tycoon he had represented himself to be.

The door before which I stood had a small round mirror set at about eye level. There was no name above the bell. I rang.

A sound somewhere, so faint that I could not tell whether it came from beyond that door, or from the restaurant downstairs, or from somewhere in the street. I rang again. Knocked.

"Colin."

No answer. And yet somehow I was suddenly sure that he stood on the other side of that heavily varnished door, looking out at me through that round one-way mirror. Was there a malicious smile on that well-cut mouth with the full underlip? Or was he too furious for any sort of smile, furious that I had tracked him to this Soho restaurant?

I felt a sudden unease. But then, I had always felt that way around Colin, even when I was eleven and he—already a full adult in my eyes—had been nineteen. And that was strange because I should have had a preadolescent crush on him. Even then he had been superlatively handsome, with the sort of lush good looks that, these days, characterize male models for designer jeans.

Perhaps it was my sense of him standing behind that door. Perhaps it was a suddenly more actute awareness that I was alone in a not very savory part of a strange city. Whatever the reason, my uneasiness sharpened into fear. I went swiftly back along the hallway and down the stairs.

6

TWO

The last of the daylight had gone. The doorman stood at the curb, greeting the occupants of still another taxicab. As I turned left and hurried toward Piccadilly Circus with its busy traffic and brightly lighted shop windows and short-order restaurants, I felt a stab of guilt about the young Indian. If Colin really had been standing behind that door back there, furious because I had tracked him down, what would he do if he learned his employee had directed me to that staircase? At the very least, he would fire him. Well, all I could do was hope that the Indian had sense enough to deny that I had even approached him.

I hurried on through the polyglot crowd. Now and then an opening door let a burst of music out onto the sidewalk—a schmaltzy violin from a Hungarian restaurant, the heavy throb of a drum from a strip joint, and, from that rhythm-and-blues cellar café, an old Bill Haley number, "Rock Around the Clock."

I would go to the police the first thing tomorrow morning, I decided. Until now I had been reluctant to do so for two reasons. First, I had nothing to report to them except my own fears. After all, it was not illegal for an eighteen-year-old girl to take a trip to England alone. Second, I knew how furious my sister would be if I set the police to looking for her. Nevertheless, I would go to them.

It was only seconds after I came to that decision that the two men appeared.

They fell into step with me, one on each side. I looked at the one on my right. Late twenties, thinning brown hair, sharp-featured face scarred with what once must have been a severe case of acne. He smiled, revealing a gap where a lower front tooth should have been. "Out for a little fun, dear?"

I looked to my left. The other man was older, fatter, shorter, with an olive-complexioned face that looked vaguely Middle Eastern. "A nice drink, first of all?"

Just keep walking, I told myself. I faced forward, eyes scanning the sidewalk crowd in hope of spotting a policeman's helmet.

Only a few yards ahead was an alley. I'd thrown a swift glance down it as, minutes before, I had walked toward Colin's restaurant. It had appeared to be empty.

In New York, even screaming pedestrians were sometimes dragged off sidewalks into areaways or deserted building sites. But surely nothing like that could happen here.

The short, dark man grasped my arm just above the elbow. I halted. "Let go," I said loudly.

The thin man seized my other arm. Again he gave me a gap-toothed smile. "Now why can't we all be friendly-like?"

I opened my mouth, drew in air. But before I could scream a third voice said, "Hop it, both of you."

I looked at the man confronting us. So did my accosters. "I mean it," he said. "Hop it, while you still can."

He didn't look like a policeman, even a plainclothes one. And although he appeared reasonably fit, he was no Arnold Schwarzenegger. Nevertheless, the gap-toothed man and his companion let go of me almost simultaneously. Without a word, they turned around and walked away.

The third man said, "Where are you going?"

My voice trembled slightly. "To the Piccadilly Circus bus stop."

"I had best come with you."

We walked in silence for a few seconds. Then he said, "You don't look daft."

I made no reply. True, I had reason to be grateful to him. But that gave him no right to be rude.

"Even an American girl should have been able to see that this is not a good neighborhood for solitary sight-seeing."

So he had spotted my American accent. Well, that was no great feat. And because of all that public television watching, I had been able to tell not just that he was an Englishman but also that he was a Londoner, and a Cockney.

He went on, "What are you doing in Soho?"

I had no intention of confiding my family troubles to a

stranger. I studied him from the corner of my eye. Blond. About thirty. A good-looking and vaguely familiar face with a sleepy droop to the eyelids. A well-built body, dressed rather formally in dark trousers, a blue shirt and darker blue tie, and a gray jacket. With his face in profile to me, I could not be sure of the color of his eyes, but I had caught the impression that they were gray-blue.

I said belatedly, "Oh, just wandering around."

A certain prickliness in my voice must have decided him to drop the subject. He looked down at me. Yes, his eyes were gray-blue.

"What's your name?"

"Carr. Jennifer Carr. But I'm called Jenny."

"Missouri? Tennessee?"

I felt astonished. It was one thing for him to recognize an American accent. It was quite another to pin it down to a particular small region.

"Missouri," I admitted, "down in the southeast corner where it borders Tennessee. How did you know?"

"Oh, I've knocked about the States a bit. Rock-climbing mostly, in various places, including the Ozarks. And I've always had an ear for accents. So what is a Missouri girl doing alone after dark in Soho?"

"I answered that."

We passed another bookshop where in the brightly lighted interior readers stood in lonely absorption. "Incidentally," I said, "what did you come up here for? A browse through the bookshops?"

He smiled. "Not my cup of tea. No, I'm here because of my job."

I looked at him questioningly.

"I'm a journalist. A reporter, you Yanks usually say. I just came from an interview with a Saudi who's opened a new gambling house in Soho. By the way, my name is Mike. Mike Baker."

"Mike for Michael?"

"That's right."

Suddenly I knew why his face seemed familar. "You look quite a lot like Michael Caine, you know."

"Never heard of him."

His tone as well as his words told me that he was tired of people commenting on the resemblance.

We had reached Piccadilly Circus. He said, as we walked toward a queue of people at the bus stop, "Where are you going?"

"Ebury Street."

"Bed-sitter?"

"Yes." A Londoner, of course, would know about that region near Victoria Station where old houses had been converted into inexpensive hostelries.

"Might as well do it right," he said as we joined the queue. "Wait with you until your bus comes, I mean."

As I stood silently beside this handsome though some-what sardonic man, I found myself hoping that it would be a good long while before my bus appeared. But it lumbered up to the stop almost immediately. He handed me onto the back step. I looked down into the sleepy-eyed face. I was all ready to say, "McBrady House. It's fifth from the corner of Ebury and Victoria Streets."

But of course he had to ask first.

He didn't ask. Maybe he was afraid I wouldn't answer

the question. Maybe he was not interested. Anyway, he didn't ask.

"I'm afraid I haven't really thanked you," I said.

He just nodded. Then, as the bus began to move, "Goodbye, Jenny."

THREE

McBrady House was only a few yards from the Ebury Street bus stop. I went up the steps and through the entrance, which, Mrs. Ryan had said, was left unlocked only until eleven o'clock. After that you had to ring.

The entrance hall, with its carpet so worn that you couldn't tell whether its floral design was of roses or peonies or just what, smelled faintly of cabbage. When I had been admitted to this establishment that morning, gritty-eyed from a sleepless night on the plane, Mrs. Ryan had disclaimed all responsibility for the aroma. "I might be Irish, but I never cook cabbage. Never. It was Mrs. McBrady, the woman I leased this place from. She must have cooked it for every meal, from breakfast to high tea, because no matter what I do I can't get the smell out."

I climbed the stairs. Unlike the worn carpet and the cabbage smell, the broad staircase with its fine ebony banister evoked the long-ago days when this rooming house must have been the town residence of some private family.

My room—really two small rooms, a foyer–sitting room and a bedroom—was on the second floor, third on the right, just past the pay telephone affixed to the wall. I unlocked the door, switched on the thriftily dim overhead light in the foyer with its small settee and its electric hot plate on a table against one wall, and went into the bedroom. I placed my shoulder bag on the washstand. There were "facilities" down the hall, one room with a basin and an enormous bathtub, and, in a separate room, an ancient pull-chain toilet with a tank of golden oak above it. But Mrs. Ryan also had provided this room with its own washstand, complete with a tall china pitcher and basin ornamented with roses.

In the mirror above the washstand I looked at my reflection. My freckles were almost invisible in that dim light. It seemed to me that my face looked thinner. That wasn't surprising. Last night on the plane, and for several indecision-torn days before that, I had not had much appetite.

What had Michael Baker thought of my severely plain skirt and shirt, and my face ornamented with its freckles? Had he still considered me at least a little attractive? Or had my appearance, like my presence in Soho, made him feel I must be some kind of a nut?

I undressed, put on a nightgown and a blue flannel robe. Then, carrying a towel, washcloth, tooth powder, and toothbrush, I visited the facilities down the hall. When I returned to my room I did not turn on the bedside lamp, even though, at my request, Mrs. Ryan had replaced a low-wattage globe with one strong enough for reading. Those few minutes outside Colin's door, and later on that encounter with the sidewalk toughs, must have been even harder on my nerves than I had realized at the time, because now I felt exhausted. I turned back the pink rayon coverlet and two thin blankets on the bed, switched off the light, and slid between the sheets.

Refracted light from a street lamp below my window struck through the thin curtain and gleamed on the water pitcher's rounded side. Suddenly I remembered that the house in which I grew up contained several such pitchers. Not in any of the bedrooms. Years ago, probably even before my father was born, someone had carried those old pitchers and washbasins up to the attic.

That house had not been the one built by my great-great-grandfather. His white-pillared mansion of red brick, set in the midst of cotton fields, had remained in the Carr family only until the early 1920s. It was then that my grandfather, financially unable to keep the place up, had sold it to some rich northerners who subsequently turned the cotton fields into pastureland for thoroughbred horses. With the proceeds from the sale, my grandfather bought one of Carrsville's two drugstores. He also bought a house on the town's Main Street, a rambling 1880 gray-frame with cupolas and wraparound porch. Judging by the size of the house, he had expected to have a large family, but as it turned out my father grew up there as an only child. And not long after his father's death, he had brought a pretty blond bride to live there with him.

It had never occurred to me to regret that the Carrs no longer owned that *Gone with the Wind*–style mansion set in its spacious fields. All through my childhood and teenage years, I thoroughly enjoyed being a town girl.

True, there were unhappy intervals. When I was seven my week-old baby brother died. Young as I was, I could

15

feel my parents' desolation like an almost physical weight upon my small body. But sixteen months later my sister—named Elizabeth, but from the first called Betsy—was born, and the shadow that had lain over our house for more than a year seemed to lift.

Somehow I never felt for my sister the jealous competitiveness that textbooks call sibling rivalry. Perhaps it was because of the fairly wide age gap between us. Perhaps it was because, even before she was a year old, she had developed a prettiness irresistible to everyone, including me. Whereas I, with my red-brown hair and my eyes of almost the same shade, resembled our father, Betsy had inherited our mother's curly blond hair and blue eyes and small, even features. What was more, the iris of her right eye had a wedge-shaped fleck of green. It gave a touch of strangeness to what otherwise might have been a too-perfect prettiness. By the time I was eleven and Betsy was three, I was so proud of her, so pleased to see the admiration in others' faces when I led her along the elm-shaded sidewalks, that I think my feeling for her was more maternal than sisterly.

It was during my eleventh summer that my mother and sister and I went to visit an aunt I had never seen, Evelyn Bracely, and her son Colin. Several years my mother's senior, Aunt Evelyn had married an army lieutenant just before the Korean War, a conflict from which he had emerged with a Silver Star. While he rose to captain, then major, then colonel, she and their son had moved with him from one army base to another. Finally, as a major general, he was assigned to New Jersey's Fort Dix. With his retirement near, he and Aunt Evelyn had looked around for a permanent place to live. Unable to find a house near the fort that suited both their taste and their income, they finally settled on a condominium in Queens, even though it would be a long commute to New Jersey.

Less than six months after they bought the condominium, Roger Bracely, who in Korea had wiped out a Chinese machine-gun nest singlehandedly, was stabbed to death by a fifteen-year-old mugger on a Manhattan subway platform.

Because my mother did not believe in taking children to funerals, and because my father was working twelve hours a day at the Carr Pharmacy without assistance, my mother flew east alone for Roger Bracely's last rites. She had been back in Carrsville only a few weeks when my Aunt Evelyn, near hysteria, telephoned. She couldn't "adjust" to life without Roger, she said. And she was having "considerable difficulties" with Colin. Would my mother please come to her for the summer?

"You could bring both girls," my mother quoted her as saying. "Back here there are lots of things for children of all ages to do during the summer."

We talked it over at dinner that night, seated at the round table beneath the droplight with its octagonal shade of green glass. My mother said, "Dan, I don't want to leave you alone, not even for a few weeks."

"Now why not? It's plain that Evelyn needs you. Besides, for years now you've been talking about how wonderful it would be to spend a few weeks in New York."

"If you could go—"

"You know I can't afford to close the drugstore for even a little while."

"Yes, I know. But I don't think I should go without you."

"For heaven's sake, Molly. I'm a grown boy."

"Darling, it's your ulcer. You know what Dr. Barnes says. If you don't stick to your diet . . ."

My father almost never swore, not even mildly. But now he said, "Damn it all, Molly. If you want to make my ulcer worse, just go on treating me as if I'm an invalid."

Dessert spoon in her mouth, Betsy looked at him with gleefully shocked eyes. "Ooh! Daddy said a bad word."

"Be quiet, Betsy." My mother's voice was sharp. Then she looked at my father, her blue eyes filled with both hurt and anxiety. "I don't want to make you feel like an invalid. It's just that . . ."

It was just that he was so very dear to her. I knew that she loved Betsy and me. But always I had sensed that my father was the one great love of her life.

She turned to me. "How do you feel about it, Jenny? Do you want to visit your Aunt Evelyn in Queens this summer?"

Perhaps surprisingly, I wasn't keen on the idea. As I've said, I liked being a town girl. I'd looked forward to my small-town summer. Swimming in the district high school pool, which each summer was thrown open to grade-school kids. Playing run-sheep-run in the warm early darkness, heart pounding with a sense of real peril even though it was only a game. Too, perhaps I'd be able to help out in the drugstore, as I had some Saturdays during the past year. I'd liked the mingled smells of eau de cologne and aspirin and hair tonic. And I'd liked it that people still commented on the resemblance between us, even though my father's hair was now more gray than red-brown.

But still—Radio City Music Hall and the Rockettes.

The Statue of Liberty and the Empire State Building. "Yes, I guess I want to go."

"*I* want to go! I want to see the queen!"

"Queens, Betsy," my mother said. "It's a place, not a person. All right, we'll go."

Aunt Evelyn's apartment, six rooms opening onto a long hall in an old brick building on a quiet street, was in no way remarkable. In its living room a sofa and two armchairs upholstered in dark blue velour stood on pearl-gray wall-to-wall carpeting. Dark blue draperies framed windows overlooking a courtyard with shaded benches set along cement walks. No apartment could have appeared more ordinary, more solidly middle-class. And yet from the first I had a sense of something oppressive in the atmosphere. At first I thought the cause must be my aunt's grief for her husband. Later I realized that I must also have sensed her constant unease over her only child.

Colin did not appear until five days after my mother and Betsy and I arrived in Queens. He had "taken a trip with friends," Aunt Evelyn had told us. When he finally did show up, he appeared at first like a son to make any mother's heart swell with pride. With dark, loosely waving hair, large brown eyes, and regular features, he might have been a movie star back in the days when movie stars looked like Tony Curtis, not Dustin Hoffman. For a nineteen-year-old, his manners were amazingly smooth. He seemed friendly to Betsy and me and downright courtly to my mother. But with a child's sure instinct I recognized the falsity of his surface manner. And only a few days after his return home I learned what he was really like.

That afternoon I had thought myself alone in the apartment. Colin was out somewhere, and my mother and Aunt Evelyn and Betsy had gone down to enjoy the sunshine in the courtyard. To finish a letter to my father, I had stayed behind in the bedroom I shared with Betsy. Then, finding I had no stamp, I went to the living room to look in the desk between the two long windows. Colin had entered the apartment without my hearing him. He stood looking at his father's portrait above the small fireplace. Only a few years ago, Aunt Evelyn had told us, she'd had the portrait painted from a photograph, one taken not long after her husband had won the Silver Star.

Colin stood in profile to me, hands clasped behind his back, gaze fixed on the painting of the uniformed man who, at the time the photograph was taken, had been less than thirty. Colin's face was filled with such hatred that I stopped in my tracks.

He turned his head. After a moment he smiled, but the malevolence was still there in the handsome face. "Hello, Jenny." Then, after a pause: "Jenny! How come they stuck you with a Missouri hillbilly name like that?"

The smooth-mannered adult of the past few days was gone now. Instead he seemed like some malicious boy of my own age or even younger. I could have pointed out that my real name was Jennifer. But I wasn't going to make any concessions. "I like being Jenny," I said, "and I like being a Missourian."

"So did my old man. God, what a nerd." He looked back at the portrait. "You know how he got that piece of tin pinned to his chest?"

"He got it for being brave."

"For being a ding-a-ling, you mean. Crawled out of his foxhole at night and wiped out a gook machine-gun crew, all by himself. Why he wasn't killed, nobody knows. And what did he get for it besides a medal? Years of dragging himself and Mom and me from one army post to another. And then, just when he's about to collect his pension, what happens?" He laughed. "Some spick kid sticks a knife into him."

I blurted, "You hate him, don't you?"

"Damned right! Even when I was a little kid he was telling me I must go to West Point. Carry on the tradition, he said. God! You'd have thought he was descended from Lighthorse Harry Lee instead of a long line of Missouri farmers. Anyway, by the time I was fourteen he saw he'd better give up that idea."

I wondered why. Because Colin had gotten into some kind of trouble that made him ineligible for West Point?

He went on. "By the time I was seventeen I was making more money some months than he did in a whole year. He raised hell about it, said I'd disgraced him and all that bull. Truth was, he was jealous because I had the kind of brains and guts he didn't have, the kind that makes money."

He looked at me, and again his smile was that of a nasty ten-year-old. "I hope you've got brains, kid."

I said nothing.

"You're going to need them to make a living. No guy will want to be *your* meal ticket, not with those freckles you've got."

I could have told him that, freckles or no freckles, I'd received a respectable number of valentines last February. And on May Day five little baskets of flowers had been left on our doorstep. Instead I cried, "Go fly a kite!" and went into my room and slammed the door.

I told no one of that conversation with Colin. I like to

think that, young as I was, I felt an obligation to shield my aunt from the knowledge of her son's behavior toward me. But I think that the compelling reason was a selfish one. I feared that if my mother realized what sort of young man Colin was, she'd want to take Betsy and me home. And I'd begun to enjoy the visit. I enjoyed the boat trip around Manhattan, the city's soaring towers set with windows that sparkled like diamonds. And although I didn't like the zoo much—too many of the animals looked sad— I did like the aquarium, where the dolphins seemed to enjoy displaying their acrobatic leaps the length of the long pool. Most of all I liked the Rockettes. Betsy did, too, so much so that my mother the next day took us to a performance of *The Sleeping Beauty* and, a few days later, to a children's ballet based on the Hansel and Gretel story.

Much as I enjoyed the ballets, I had neither hope nor desire that someday I might whirl across a stage on the points of my toes. Betsy, however, announced loudly more than once that she was going to be a dancer.

It was toward the end of our stay with Aunt Evelyn that I heard her talking about Colin. I had been down in the courtyard, reading on a bench while Betsy and several of her contemporaries played tag. Finally a little girl with red pigtails asked me to read to them. Since I didn't think Nancy Drew would interest three- to five-year-olds, I went upstairs to get one of Betsy's picture books. I was about to leave when I heard my mother and Aunt Evelyn come into the next room, probably from the kitchen.

". . . just can't understand," Aunt Evelyn was saying, "how our son, *Roger's* son—" She broke off. "Sometimes

22

I'm actually afraid of him. Sometimes I'm sure he's psychopathic."

I stood there uneasily. It was obvious that they didn't know I had come back to the apartment. Should I make some sort of noise? But that would embarrass them.

My mother said, "Surely you don't mean that."

"What else can you call a boy that hates his father? A boy who makes money in all sorts of ways, even dealing in drugs. Yes, Molly, I've been ashamed to tell you that, but it's true. There's been no reason for it. It's not as if Roger tried to *force* him to go to West Point. He had put money aside so that Colin could go to any college that would accept him—Oh, lord! Did we leave that oven on?"

I heard both women hurry down the hall toward the kitchen. I waited a moment, and then slipped from the bedroom and crossed the hall to the apartment's front door.

A week later we returned to Carrsville. That fall I entered the seventh grade. As for Betsy, she enrolled in not only a newly opened nursery school but in Miss Gloria Rose's Dance Academy, which offered "ballet, jazz, and tap," in Granger, a larger town ten miles away.

As I have said, ours was a happy childhood. I went through high school, not with honors but well enough, and then enrolled in Brewster College, fifteen miles from home, as an economics major. Betsy, meanwhile, had grown more enchanting by the day. I don't think grammar school boys ever teased her; they were too awed by her beauty. But far more impressive to me was her talent. When she whirled across the floor at the dance academy, or, later on, across the stage at almost every Carrsville

23

civic event, I would think: Someday people in Paris will be watching her, and in London and Rome.

Strange how suddenly the happiest family can be smashed to bits. That is what happened to us. No one knows when my father's ulcer turned to something else, something implacable and deadly. My mother, her face rigid with pain and horror, obviously could not manage alone, and so I left college.

A week after the funeral, my mother had the first of two heart attacks. The medical explanations don't matter. I knew she had just worn out.

She must have realized that, too. Only hours before her death she looked at me as I sat, numb but trying to smile, in the chair beside her hospital bed. "Oh, Jenny! I tried so hard to hold on for you and Betsy, but I just couldn't, I couldn't!"

"We'll be fine," I managed to say. "I promise you—"

"Oh, Jenny! Your college—"

In my pain I tried a small joke. "The college isn't going anywhere. It'll be there when I get back to it. And Mama, I'll take care of Betsy."

After my mother's death my sister and I continued to live in our house. It was hard to find a buyer for a house that large. And since it had no mortgage, it was cheaper to live there, with most of the rooms blanked off, than to rent an apartment. I took a job at the Carrsville National Bank, first as assistant teller and then as teller. And when Betsy turned fifteen she worked during high school vacations in a hamburger stand. Both of us thought her ballet lessons were the most important item of expense, and so those bills were paid before she contributed to the housekeeping money.

24

I dated, of course. Despite Colin's prediction, men seemed attracted to me. But some of them shied away when they realized that a commitment to me would mean a commitment to my kid sister, at least until she became fully self-supporting. Other men whom I dated just didn't appeal to me very much.

It wasn't until I reached twenty-four that I met a man I really liked. Liked well enough to think of marrying him. Liked well enough to spend several nights in his apartment. But before long I realized that we were at odds about almost everything—politics, religion, and even music. If we married, what we'd have would be bouts of irritation or anger interspersed with bouts of passion—or at least until the passion faded. I broke it off, or maybe we both did, because despite what I regarded as stubborn wrong-headedness, he too was bright enough to see we weren't suited to each other.

Sometimes I would lie awake thinking, "I'm in my middle twenties. What's going to happen to me?" Perhaps not much. Perhaps I would be like Miss Irene—her last name was Flint—who had worked in the bank for thirty-two years and no doubt would go on working there until she dropped. Or like Donna White in the beauty parlor, who, at the age of forty, had married a man who was supposed to be a carpenter but who went hunting or fishing nearly every day, leaving her to earn their living among the hair dryers.

It seemed to me that life had been even more unfair to Betsy. *She* was the talented one. But her ballet teacher had said that she had taught my sister everything she herself knew. And there was no money to send Betsy to classes in St. Louis or Kansas City.

25

What was more, I had a dismayed feeling that my sister, at least partly because of my encouragement, would never be content to settle for marriage to some local boy, no matter how attractive or hardworking or ambitious.

Carrsville, the little town that during our childhoods had seemed to rock us like a cradle, had turned into a trap.

Our Aunt Evelyn's death, when it came, was no great surprise. Her occasional letters had mentioned ill health. Because Betsy, fresh out of high school, had just begun a job in a small electronics plant on the town's edge, I flew back to the funeral alone.

To my amazement, Colin was not among the people—friends and neighbors as well as relatives of Aunt Evelyn's late husband—gathered in a small funeral chapel. A sister of Roger Bracely, sounding embarrassed, told me that "Colin's abroad somewhere, and I guess they couldn't reach him."

I started home late that afternoon, traveling by jet, then a commuter plane, and then my old Chevy, which I'd left at the small airport near Carrsville.

Betsy and I were having dinner in the breakfat nook the next night when the wall phone rang. I answered it.

"Miss Carr? Miss Jennifer Carr?"

"Yes."

"This is Paul Lasker. I was Mrs. Bracely's lawyer."

"Oh, yes." Aunt Evelyn had mentioned him once or twice in her letters. "Were you at the funeral? I didn't see—"

"No, I have a terrible cold." He sounded like it. "But if I had known you planned to leave so soon I would have managed to get there somehow. You see, I must talk to you about your aunt's will."

"Her will?"

"You and your sister are named in it."

Feeling a rush of affection, I wondered what Aunt Evelyn had left me. Her four-strand crystal necklace? I'd admired that very much when I was eleven years old. Perhaps she had left her cultured pearl ring to Betsy.

"That was very kind of my aunt."

"I think it could be called more than kind, Miss Carr. She left you and your sister everything she possessed."

I said, after a stunned moment, "But that can't be. Her son—"

"There is a clause about him in her will. Mrs. Bracely stated, 'My son having exceeded the bounds of all forgiveness, I hereby bequeath him the sum of one dollar.' "

What on earth could he have done, I wondered, to make his mother turn her back on him so completely?

"Now, it is no great fortune," Mr. Lasker was saying. "Much of her money was in annuities, and so passed out of her estate at her death. But she did leave around sixty thousand in cash, plus the apartment, of course."

I stood speechless. He went on, "There will be papers to sign. How soon can you get back to New York?"

I managed to say, "Three days. A week at most."

"Fine. When you get here, just look me up in the book. Good night, Miss Carr."

He hung up. After a moment I did, too. Betsy stared at me from the breakfast nook. "For Pete's sake, Jenny, what happened?"

"How would you like to go to New York right now and start to become a great dancer?"

"Jenny, what on—"

"Probably we'll find you don't need any more training. All you'll have to do is go to a tryout."

Betsy rose threateningly from her chair. "Jenny, if you don't—"

I threw my arms around her then and told her.

She said dazedly, "We'll quit our jobs?"

"Of course! We have an apartment and sixty thousand dollars waiting for us in Queens. What do we need with these jobs?"

"And the house?"

"Maybe we'll try to sell it sometime soon. Or maybe we'll come back here to rest whenever you've finished your world tours." I was joking about that, but not much.

"Anyway, for right now we'll just turn the key in the lock and walk away."

FOUR

Lying there in my Ebury Street room, I heard Big Ben strike eleven, each bronze stroke lingering in the late-summer dark. At the curb below my window one of those lumbering red buses came to a halt. Perhaps because of the difference in size, they seemed noisier than the one-decker green buses that ran near that apartment in Queens.

We spent our first week there getting settled, signing papers in Mr. Lasker's office, and shopping carefully. Fortunately neither of us was clothes-mad. If we had been, we realized as we wandered along the aisles of Bloomingdale's, we could easily have blown our thirty thousand apiece in a few weeks.

Besides, we had agreed that a trip to Europe would be preferable to fur coats. And so a few days after our arrival in New York we applied for passports.

With a vast sense of worldliness, we read copies of

Variety from front page to last, making note of future calls for dancers. We also phoned several ballet companies. None of them was holding tryouts at the moment.

It was during our first week in Queens that I learned why we, not Colin Bracely, had become his mother's heirs. "Everything in that apartment is now yours," Mr. Lasker had assured us. Before I even looked through the closets—filled with clothes that we would give away, since they would not fit either of us—I opened the top drawer of a mahogany dresser in her bedroom. It was there that she had kept her white leather case of modest jewelry, the jewelry I had loved to try on that summer when I was eleven.

The case was still there. On top of the crystal necklace and the pearl ring and some coral bracelets lay a folded note. I opened it, knowing it must be for me. Otherwise she would not have left it in that particular place. She had written:

Dear Jenny,
    You and Betsy are both young and soft-hearted. It might be that my son could prevail upon you to give him some of the money I intend to leave you. And he must never touch that money. It was money that Roger earned by hard work, and devotion to duty, and sometimes at the risk of his life.
    I have just learned that for several years now Colin has been doing something that I cannot possibly forgive. He has been helping run illegal arms to whoever will buy them—terrorists, mercenaries, enemies of his own country, *anyone*. No telling how

much he has made out of explosives which blasted innocent people to bits in Belfast, London, Rome, North Africa.

He knows that even though I could forgive him for other things—drug-dealing, for instance—I would never forgive *that*, not in his father's son. He knew that would devastate me completely. That was why he told me of it. Oh, he was clever about it. He didn't give me a shred of proof to take to the police. If I'd gone to them, he would have been able to portray me as a somewhat balmy old lady. But he wanted to be sure I knew what he'd been doing.

If Betsy is with you when you find this note, she will of course have to know about it. But otherwise, don't let anyone know. It could only harm Roger Bracely's memory. Colin can't be stopped without some sort of evidence. We can only hope that in time justice of one sort or another will catch up with him.

Watch out for him! It would be terrible indeed if by leaving you a little money I have brought you into danger. So have nothing to do with him, if possible.

All my love,
Aunt Evelyn

I reread the note, thinking how strange it was that someone who had grown up in this prosaic middle-class apartment could have anything to do with sprawled limbs and screaming sirens at the Athens airport or a market-place in Beirut.

31

Laying the note aside, I began to take out the jewelry piece by piece. When the box was unpacked I saw that something rectangular lay beneath the thin blue paper on the bottom. I took it out. It was a color snapshot of Colin leaning against a long, foreign-looking sports car. The building behind him, only part of which had been caught by the camera, also had a foreign look. Above its doorway gilded letters said: "Café Ambr—"

I turned the snapshot over. On the reverse side someone, presumably Colin, had written, "The car and the restaurant are both mine." Below that, small stamped letters read: "Crown Photo Developers, Sloane Square, London, SW I."

Feeling about Colin as she did, why had Aunt Evelyn saved that snapshot with its boastful message? Perhaps because in spite of everything she still felt some love for her handsome son. Or perhaps it had given her some faint hope for him. Restaurant-keeping is at least a lawful enterprise.

I replaced the snapshot in the box, picked up Aunt Evelyn's note. I walked down the long hall to the kitchen, burned the note in the sink, and washed the ashes down the drain. When Betsy came home—she had been at the hairdresser—I did not tell her about the note. Our aunt hadn't wanted me to. Besides, surely my sister did not need a warning against Colin. We had both grown up knowing that our cousin belonged behind bars.

On our sixth day in New York we went to our first audition—or cattle call, as *Variety* had taught us to say. In an alley that ran alongside a Manhattan theater, at least fifty girls had lined up in front of a table that filled most of a doorway. I leaned against a wall, warmed by the sunlight that penetrated the alley, and surely feeling as excited as Betsy herself.

A man emerged from the theater and sat down at the table. The line began to move, each girl telling the man something—her name, I suppose—and then turning into the building. When the last of them had gone inside I lingered there for several minutes. We had agreed that I was to wait for her in a pizza place half a block away. But now I felt that I couldn't stand the suspense.

The man and the table had disappeared, but another man, an older one, sat in a chair just inside the doorway. I walked over to him. "Would it be all right if I—"

"Sorry, miss. You should have signed up when you could. No one else can go in now."

"I'm not a dancer. It's my sister. This is her first tryout, and I'd so very much like to watch her."

"I don't make the rules, young lady."

"But how could I do any harm? You were here when the girls lined up, weren't you?"

"That's right."

"Maybe you remember my sister. She's blond and rather small, and she has big blue eyes with a green fleck in the right one."

"Yes, I remember her." He studied me. "Awfully proud of your sister, aren't you?"

I nodded.

He got to his feet. "Well, come inside." He led me across a dimly lighted space, its floor littered with two battered desks and a coil of rope, to a door. "Go through there and straight up the aisle to the back of the theater. Sit in the last row. And when you leave, be just as quiet about it."

33

On the other side of the door an aisle, dimly lighted and thickly carpeted, sloped upward past ranks of empty seats. I was aware of light and sound on the stage to my left, but I did not look that way. Instead I scuttled as quickly as possible toward the back row. When I reached it I slipped into the aisle seat.

Up on the stage a man sat at an upright piano. The same man who had been out in the alley sat at a table, an opened notebook before him. Dozens of girls in practice clothes did stretching exercises, chattered to each other, or merely rested their weight on one foot and looked bored. I could see Betsy. In her pink leotard, she was chatting with a tall girl of about her own age in green. Down in the orchestra's third row sat a man and a woman.

A few more girls came on stage from the wings. Then the man at the table said, "All of us here? OK, let's line up, a dozen at a time. No, I count fourteen. The girl at each end should step back. That's right. Now, what I want to see for this first round is just a simple time step."

Betsy had lined up with the first twelve. My sister was about to perform on a stage. Not a stage at Miss Gloria Rose's Academy, or one at the Elks' convention, but a stage in Manhattan, the theatrical capital of the world.

Aware of my quickened pulse rate, I heard the pianist launch into the title song from *Forty-second Street*, heard the rhythmic beat of tap shoes. When the pianist had played perhaps ninety seconds, the man sitting down in the shadowy orchestra said, "Hold it! The girl on the left end—yes, you—and the girl with the pigtails, please step aside. That will be all, and thank you very much. All right, Barney."

The piano started up again. The girls, ten of them now, resumed their rhythmic tapping. Those two other girls, poor things, had been turned down, but Betsy—

"Hold it! The girl with the bandanna headband and the blond girl in the pink leotard, that will be all and thank you very much. All right, let's try it again."

I saw Betsy's stricken face before she turned and walked quickly toward the wings. For a moment I sat rigid. Then, terrified that she might learn that I had witnessed her rejection, I scuttled down the aisle.

The old man beside the stage door, looking up from his newspaper, asked no question. I guess he didn't need to. " 'Bye, miss," he said as I neared the door. I nodded and went out into the alley.

When Betsy came into the pizza parlor a long twenty minutes later, her eyes were reddened. I said, in a carefully casual voice, "How did it go?"

"Oh, Jenny! They didn't want me!"

"Really? I wonder why." For twenty minutes I had been asking myself why they should reject Betsy, obviously the most graceful and attractive girl there, and had come up with several answers. "Maybe they were looking for girls with just tap and jazz training. You really are basically a classical dancer, you know."

She brightened a little. "That's true. And I thought of something else. It might be that one or more of the principals is blond, and so they don't want too many blondes in the chorus."

I nodded. "That's possible. Besides, you're awfully young, Betsy, and you look even younger. That's all right for the ballet, but perhaps not for musical comedy. Well, it won't do any harm to go to a few more chorus calls, but I don't think we should count on anything until the ballet tryouts."

A few days later, tired of idleness, I started looking for a job. Once Betsy's career was well launched, I would go back to college. But in the meantime, I might as well make money. My half of that sixty thousand dollars, vast as it had seemed in Carrsville, wasn't going to last forever, not in New York. Looking over the want ads, I saw that I could have my choice. I could try for a glamour job at a minuscule salary in advertising or publishing or TV, or I could make nearly twice as much if I decided to forgo glamour. I finally went to work as the sole clerical employee of Mr. Lee Park, a fortyish Korean who ran a print shop on the West Side.

As for Betsy, she still had not found employment. But she had managed to make friends at some of the auditions, friends who invited her to parties and for evenings at various discos. Uneasy about her—after all, she had just turned eighteen—I asked questions about these new friends. Were any of them into coke?

"Some are. And of course a lot of them use pot." She laughed. "You're not worried about me, are you? Why, no dancer with the brains of a flea would fool around with stuff like that."

Obviously, she meant it. Feeling a little ashamed of my anxieties, I relaxed.

One July morning I arrived at the print shop to find it a shambles. A pipe in the apartment upstairs had burst during the night and sent water cascading down on presses, office furniture, and piles of paper. I might as well go home, Mr. Park told me. It would take all day for him and the workmen he'd summoned to clean up the mess.

Instead of going back to the Queens apartment, I went to a raincoat sale at a store on Broadway. Toward noon, carrying my package, I wandered up Columbus Avenue past the trendy cafés and deli shops and boutiques. Suddenly I stopped short. Ahead of me, seated at a sidewalk café table, Betsy was smiling across a tall glass at Colin Bracely. Even though I had not seen him for fifteen years, I was sure it was Colin, not only from my childhood memory of him but from that snapshot in his mother's jewelry box.

Colin Bracely and my young sister. Here on this sunlit, noisy street, with pedestrians hurrying past me and Bruce Springsteen's voice issuing from a nearby record store, I felt strangely chilled.

Then Betsy caught sight of me and made a jerky movement that almost upset her glass. "Why—why, Jenny!" Her face, always so revealing, was filled with guilt.

Smiling, Colin got to his feet. "So it's Jenny, all grown up." He pulled out a chair. "Join us, won't you?"

I looked at him stonily. How old was he now? Thirty-three? Thirty-four? Somewhere in there. He looked it, and maybe a little more. True, his body appeared trim as a twenty-year-old's in jeans and an open-necked blue sports shirt, and his hair was still dark and thick and wavy. But there was a slackness around the eyes and the full mouth, something that brought the word *corruption* to mind.

I said, "How is it you're with my sister?"

"Now, now, Jenny! You wouldn't want to make a scene, would you? Better sit down."

He was right. A scene wouldn't help. I sank into the chair he drew out for me. He asked what I wanted, and then relayed my order for a Campari and soda to the hovering waiter.

When the waiter had gone I looked at Betsy. Resentment had replaced the guilt in her face. She said, before I could ask, "I ran into Colin three weeks ago, and then again a week later. He called up this morning, just to ask how I was. I told him I was going to an audition at an off-off-Broadway theater on Amsterdam, so he suggested that we meet here around noon."

There was no need for me to ask how the audition had gone. If it had turned out well, she would have told me.

Colin said, amusement in his voice, "If you're wondering why she didn't tell you we'd renewed our old acquaintance, it's because she knew you'd inherited my mother's dim view of me, along with her money." He added quickly, "Not that I hold it against you two—being out of her will, I mean. In all modesty, I can assure you that for me that kind of money is pretty small change."

Was he telling the truth? Perhaps.

The waiter set my drink down before me. When he had gone I asked, "What sort of business are you in?"

"I own a café in London. I'm over here now to look at some other properties."

Was the café the one in that snapshot? Probably. But I wondered how many other and less legitimate sources of income he had.

"Incidentally," he went on, "I ran into Betsy at a disco. The Red Parrot, wasn't it, Betsy? I saw this blonde with

38

a green fleck in one of her big blue eyes and I thought, 'Good Lord, it can't be that three-year-old my Aunt Molly brought to New York.' But when I asked her she said yes, she was Betsy Carr."

"And the second time we ran into each other it was at another disco." My sister's voice held lingering defensiveness.

"Colin!"

I turned to look at a man who had stopped on the sidewalk. He was of average height and olive complexion, and I judged his age to be about forty-five. Despite partial baldness, he was handsome in a way that suggested Latin origins, or perhaps Greek or even Turkish. Especially considering the casual attire prevalent in this yuppie neighborhood, he was expensively, even foppishly dressed in a suit of gray-slubbed silk.

"Tony!" Colin had sprung to his feet. As the two men greeted each other, I had a puzzled sense that they were only pretending to be surprised at their meeting.

"Girls," Colin said, "this is Antonio Braselmo. I'm staying in his apartment while I'm here in New York. Tony, these are my cousins, Jenny and Betsy Carr. Will you join us?"

"With young ladies so beautiful, need you ask?" I did not know enough about foreign accents to place his. It might have been almost anything.

He sat down, ordered a drink, and then smiled directly at me. "You will allow me to buy luncheon?"

I did not want to have lunch here. And yet I didn't like to leave Betsy alone with these two men, especially when I had this uneasy feeling that their meeting here had been prearranged. . . .

39

"What is the trouble?" Mr. Braselmo asked. "Is it that you have employment you must return to?"

Before I thought, I said, "No, I have the day off."

"Then why not lunch with us, Miss Carr?"

"Oh, for heaven's sake, Jenny!" Colin said. "If there's something you'd rather do, run along. At one-thirty I'll send Betsy home. I have to, because I have a business appointment then."

"Yes, I'll be fine," Betsy said.

I could see that my obvious hostility toward Colin and my mistrust of both him and his friend had not only irritated her, it had embarrassed her, too. And probably I *had* been making rather a fool of myself. Betsy was young, but she also was long used to masculine attention. She would not be apt to let her cousin and his middle-aged friend beguile her into anything foolish. I stood up, lifted my package, said good-bye, and walked toward the subway.

When Betsy came back to the Queens apartment in midafternoon, I was doing my nails in the living room while I watched "Jeopardy" on TV. She said, almost sullenly, "What was the idea of treating me like a fifteen-year-old?"

I'd been prepared for that. I placed my bottle of nail polish on the coffee table, switched off the TV, and then said, "There's something you don't know about Colin." I told her of the note his mother had placed in her jewelry box.

My sister said slowly, "I don't believe it."

I cried, "You think I'd lie about a thing like that?"

"Oh, no! I believe you found the note. I just don't

40

believe what was in it. I think Colin loved to torment his mother. And he told me he could get her to believe almost anything."

I considered that for a moment. It could be. Well, if he had made up that story about arms-running, it had cost him something. No matter how much money he had made in one way or another, and no matter what he might say to the contrary, surely he had regretted the loss of sixty thousand dollars and a Queens condominium.

I asked, "What did you think of that Mr. Braselmo?"

Her voice still held a sullen note. "He was all right. After lunch Colin walked with me to the subway stop, and he told me his friend was rich. Emerald mines in Colombia, among other things."

"Did he try to date you?"

"Mr. Braselmo? Sort of. I let him see I wasn't interested."

"I should think not, a man more than twice your age."

The beautiful blue eyes narrowed. "You know something, Jenny? You're a little mixed up. You're my sister, not my mommy. Now, I don't think Colin is a very nice guy, and I don't plan to see him again, although I'll probably bump into him now and then. As for Mr. Braselmo, I realize he's way too old, even for you. But let *me* make up my mind about things like that." She went down the hall. I heard the door to her room close, none too gently.

It was the nearest we had come to quarreling in all the years since our mother had died. I knew she wasn't really so very angry with me. What angered her was a world that, so far, had been blind to her talent.

In mid-August the ballet company that Betsy most aspired to held auditions, not only for prospective new members of its corps, but for prospective enrollees in the ballet school it maintained. My sister by that time must have felt considerably disheartened, because she applied only to the school.

She was turned down.

When she came home from the audition that Saturday afternoon, she went into her room, closed the door, and did not come out for almost twenty-four hours. To my amazement, when she finally did emerge she seemed quite calm, her hair drawn back into a ponytail and her tote bag over her shoulder. She was going, she said, to an audition.

When she returned her manner was much the same. She had gotten the part, she said matter-of-factly. Oh, it was no big deal. A very much off-off-Broadway production—at an old auditorium in Queens, in fact—of *Oklahoma!* She was to play the "dancing Laurie." You could never tell. It might lead to something.

I felt a half-incredulous relief. During the past few hours I had been steeling myself to face the fact that Betsy just wasn't good enough. Oh, in Carrsville she was. But in New York she had been competing with the best from every Carrsville in the nation. And she simply did not have sufficient talent for that.

Maybe, though, I had given up too soon.

The company had only two weeks to rehearse. That meant that often Betsy left the apartment before I did in the morning and did not return until six. Her manner was strange. She showed no elation, only an unnatural calm touched with grimness.

On opening night I sat with a couple of hundred other

people in a dusty auditorium built to hold several times that many. From the chatter of those around me, I gathered that nearly everyone there was a friend or relative of a cast member.

Even so, after the first-act curtain at least a third of the audience left.

From the opening moments, the performance was a disaster. The orchestra, a piano and violin and drums, played raggedly. Curly's voice was adequate, but his waistline bulged over his belt in an uncowboyish manner. All the actors but the woman playing Aunt Eller went up in their lines. By the time Betsy appeared, I was in no state to judge her performance. I felt only a numb gratitude that she got off the stage without falling down.

After the curtain's final descent, I reluctantly joined a number of others moving along a corridor backstage. Betsy stood against the wall waiting for me, her face white beneath its makeup. "We're having a meeting," she said. "You might as well go home."

Around one-thirty she returned to the apartment and walked into the kitchen, where I sat with a cup of hot chocolate. She said flatly, "Well, we've folded."

"Betsy, I'm sorry—"

"Sorry! You don't know yet how much there is to be sorry about. Thirty thousand dollars' worth of sorry, that's how much."

I said numbly, "Thirty thousand?"

"Yes! How do you think I got the part? They needed money to put the play on."

"You turned over your half of Aunt Evelyn's—"

"Yes!"

"Can't you get at least some of it back?"

"It's been spent! Costumes, lights, rent, advertising. The company's even a little in debt."

I exploded then. I don't remember all I said. But I do remember screaming, "You'll go to work! Do you understand? From now on, you'll pull your weight around here."

She turned and walked down the hall to her room.

When I left for the print shop the next morning, heavy-eyed after an almost sleepless night, she was not yet up. That afternoon when I came home I sensed something different about the apartment as soon as I entered its hall, a kind of empty feeling.

She had left a note on my dressing table. It said:

> I am going away for a while. Don't worry. And don't waste time and money trying to find me. I'll be in touch before long.
>
> I was a fool and worse. But I just couldn't help making one last grab at the dream I've had since I was—what? Four years old? Five?
>
> Take care, Jenny darling. *And don't worry.*

The note still in my hand, I stared at the wall. Where in God's name had she gone? Not back to Carrsville. She wouldn't have tried to hide that from me. She must be here in New York, staying with some of her friends. I could remember the names of some of them. My impulse was to rush to the phone book and try to look them up. But no. That might anger her, and so widen the breach between us even further. Better to wait, as she asked, until she got in touch with me.

She was all I had. Almost every waking moment during the next five days, as I traveled back and forth to my dull but well-paid job or sat alone in that apartment, she was in my thoughts. I learned then what people mean when they say that just not knowing about what has happened to a loved one is the worst torment possible.

On Saturday the airmailed picture postcard from London came. It bore the photograph of what was identified on the reverse side as the Albert Memorial. Betsy had written:

> There's a reason why I'm over here. I'm going to make up for that money I wasted, more than make up for it.
>
> I'll write again soon. And don't worry.
>
> > Love,
> > Betsy

Don't worry! She was on the other side of the Atlantic, an eighteen-year-old girl so lacking in judgment that she had turned thirty thousand dollars over to a bunch of incompetent amateurs. And she asked me not to worry.

Whom could she possibly know in London?

Colin. Colin might be back there now.

Feverishly I tried to remember the name of that man he said he'd been staying with, that handsome, balding man in the gray suit. Finally I had it. Antonio Braselmo.

I went down the hall to the kitchen and consulted the telephone book dangling beside the wall phone. Because Betsy had said he was rich, I feared that he would not be listed in the phone book. He was, though, at a Fifth Avenue address. At least there was an Antonio Braselmo there, and I doubted that the city held two men with such an odd name. I dialed.

The number I had reached, a recorded voice told me,

had been disconnected at the subscriber's request.

I hung up and stood there with my hand on the instrument, cheek pressed against the wall, eyes closed. I would go to London. It was a vast place in which to try to find anyone, but I would have to try. I couldn't stay here waiting for another overseas communication that might not ever come.

And if a letter or another card from Betsy did arrive after I left here? Well, the apartment-house manager could collect my mail for me. I could call him from London and give him a phone number. That way he could call me, out of the money I would leave him, if there was any communication from my sister.

I walked back to my bedroom and took my never-used passport from my dressing-table drawer.

Now, in my narrow bed at Mrs. Ryan's, I looked up at the shadow of a wind-stirred tree, cast onto the ceiling by a street lamp below my window.

My fault, I was thinking. Mainly my fault that my young sister's only goal in life had been to become a great dancer. My fault that, long before I finally did, I hadn't faced the fact that she lacked sufficient talent. My fault, finally, that I had made her feel she must do something desperate to make up for the money she had thrown away. To people like Betsy and me, thirty thousand dollars was indeed a lot of money. But it was nothing compared to her safety.

Don't think about it, I commanded myself. What good does it do to lie here feeling guilty?

My thoughts swerved to the evening just past. That hallway above the restaurant, and that mirrored door through which my strange cousin might or might not have been watching me. Those two creeps on that Soho sidewalk. That journalist with the sleepy-eyed poker face—

Go to sleep! I must be clear-headed for that talk with the police in the morning, so I must go to sleep.

I turned over in bed and embraced my pillow.

FIVE

The uniformed man behind the desk in the Victoria Street police substation was thin and pleasant-looking, with hair and a drooping mustache of the same ginger color. He said, "I don't want to seem unsympathetic, miss. But why are you afraid that your sister is in some kind of trouble?"

"I told you. She's just turned eighteen! And also there was her state of mind when she ran off. She'd done something terribly foolish—"

"Foolish?"

Briefly I explained to him about that disastrous production of *Oklahoma!*

"I can see, miss, how a young girl might want to run off after doing something like that. But what reason do you have to think that the police should look for her?" When I kept a baffled silence, he went on, "For that matter, how can you be sure that she came to London?"

"Why, that postcard I told you about!" I reached into my shoulder bag. "Here it is."

He looked at the Albert Memorial photograph, turned the card over, and after a moment, handed it back to me. "Mailed from London, all right. But that doesn't prove as much as you might think."

I looked at him questioningly. He said, "She might have sent it to someone over here and had him mail it for her."

"But why—"

"That way she could keep you from looking for her in New York City. Maybe it didn't occur to her that you'd cross the Atlantic to look for her."

I felt a cold dismay. Could it be that Betsy was still back in New York someplace?

I recalled one Saturday when we'd gone to a matinee on West Fifty-seventh Street. Near the theater there had been a shop with a sign that said "Wide, Wide World," or something like that. Its window had held a jumble of magazines, newspapers, and postcards from all over Europe and Asia. I imagined her going in there to buy that Albert Memorial card.

But in that case, whom had she given it to, or sent it to, to mail for her? Colin, almost certainly.

Then I said, "But surely the Immigration authorities keep records of who comes into this country. I mean, they took *my* name at Heathrow."

The ginger-haired man nodded.

"Then you could find out for me whether or not—"

"Look, miss. I'm afraid you don't understand about the police. We are empowered to undertake investigations only when there is evidence that some illegality has been committed. There is no such evidence here. There isn't even any proof that your sister has ever been in this country.

"Now, *you* can call Immigration. But don't count on getting any answer right away. Thousands of people pour into this country every day by sea and by air at literally scores of seaports and airports in England and Scotland. Especially since you don't even know the day she might have arrived, it may take them some time to tell you whether or not she ever came here.

"You can go to the American consul, of course. In fact, if I wanted to give you—what is it you Yanks call it? the brushoff?—I would advise you to do that. But I really think your consul would point out that your sister is of age to travel alone, and has a valid passport, and thus is not of concern to the consulate."

As I sat there in stricken silence he said, "Another thing you might do is to put a personal ad in one of the big circulation newspapers. If she's here, and knows you've followed her, she might feel obliged to get in touch with you. I'm sorry, miss, but that's all the advice I can give."

I thanked him and then went out into the morning sunlight. For a while I just stood against a brick wall, looking abstractedly at the people who walked past. Vaguely I was aware that most of them—matrons with shopping bags, young or youngish-looking men and women in jeans or chinos—appeared not very different from pedestrians on almost any New York street. Now and then, though, there was an impeccably tailored man, complete with bowler and tightly rolled umbrella, who seemed to me as unmistakably English as the big red buses lumbering along the street.

What if the Immigration people refused to search their records for my sister's name—refused me politely, just as that policeman had done, but still refused? Well, I *could* put a personal ad in a newspaper, but then what? Just wait and wait and wait, when she might not even be in London?

Newspapers! That newspaperman, Michael Baker, who had come to my aid the night before. Reporters had ways of cutting through red tape to get information inaccessible to ordinary people.

If only I had thought to ask him what paper he worked for. Well, if he were in the phone book, I could call him at his home in the evening.

I found that I did not want to wait until evening to find out whether or not he was listed. A telephone booth stood at the curbside about thirty feet away. I hurried to it, opened the phone book. There were eight Michael Bakers, four Michael E. Bakers, two Michael M. Bakers . . . Staring in dismay at the column of names, I again wished I had asked who employed him.

One thing seemed almost certain. A newspaper as prestigious as the *London Times* surely would not have dispatched a journalist to interview a Soho gambling-house operator. The same must hold true for publications like the *Guardian*. Probably he worked for one of those papers I had heard about, journals that in some ways were even more flamboyant than those available at supermarket checkout counters in America.

I had passed a newspaper stand about halfway between Mrs. Ryan's rooming house and the police station. I hurried back along the sidewalk to where a white-haired woman with thick legs in bright red stockings sat in a straight chair. Beside her rose a five-tier stand filled with newspapers and magazines.

"Pyeper, luv?"

"Yes, please.

"Nyetion's Dye?" Perhaps she had reached for *Nation's Day* because I was looking at it, or rather at the big-bosomed nude on its front page under the heading, "Model Charges Chiropodist with Bigamy."

I accepted the paper, paid her from the store of English pence I had obtained at the currency-exchange window at Heathrow the morning before, and then asked, "Do you mind if I copy down the names of some of your other papers?"

"No reason to mind, luv."

She watched with friendly and mildly curious eyes while in the notebook from my shoulder bag I wrote down the name of the *Thames Journal* (lead story: "Gay Sues Yugoslav Film Director for Breach of Promise"), the *Kensington Gazetteer* ("Di's Biggest Grievance Against Charles"), and several similar publications. Then I thanked her and walked rapidly back to the phone booth.

I looked up the number for the *Daily Sentinel* ("British Peer Arrested in Amsterdam Raid"). Then I studied the instructions attached to the telephone. When I felt I had mastered the dial–wait for response–deposit coin–punch button procedure, I began to call newspapers.

I was quite lucky. When I called the fourth one, the *Daily Reporter* ("Ex–Buckingham Palace Footman Arrested as Unlicensed Bookie"), and asked for Michael Baker, the switchboard operator said, "One moment, please."

Seconds later a voice I remembered said, "Baker here."

"Michael Baker?"

"Absolutely."

"This is Jenny Carr." When he didn't respond I said, "Don't you remember me? Last night—"

"I remember you."

"Would you do me a favor?"

"It depends upon what sort of favor."

He wasn't making it easy. "I think my sister flew to this country from New York not more than two weeks ago. Could you find out for sure? Find out right away?"

"Was that what you were doing in Soho? Looking for your sister?"

"Yes."

He was silent. I expected him to ask why I had thought she might be in Soho, but he did not, not then. "Better give me her name."

So he was going to help. My heart pounded. "Her name is Elizabeth Geraldine Carr, and she was born in Carrsville, Missouri."

A moment's silence. Evidently he was writing that down. "All right. I know a couple of chaps at Immigration. I should be able to find out within the next few hours."

"Then I can call you late this afternoon? Or would you rather—"

"Better that we meet for dinner. That is, if you want to tell me about this."

I found I very much wanted to meet him for dinner, and not just for the sake of enlisting his help.

"We could meet at Hal's Tavern," he was saying. "It's an old pub above a warehouse on the river. The building's been there since James the Second's time."

"How do I—"

"It's three doors from the Tower Bridge stop on the underground."

As yet I had not been down in the London subway,

which I had heard was a bewildering maze far deep in the earth.

"The food's good," he said, "and not many people come there on weeknights. I'll meet you at eight-thirty. All right?"

"All right," I said.

SIX

At the foot of the staircase, open except for a roof, which led up the side of the ancient warehouse, a sign said: "Hal's Tavern." I climbed, aware of the smell of brackish water and of the whistles of tugboats on the river. There was a door at the top of the stairs. I opened it and went in.

There was a warm mingling of lamplight and the glow of the fire that had been lit, even though the night was not really cool. A few people stood at the bar and three couples sat at tables. Michael Baker rose from a table in the far corner and stood waiting for me. His face remained almost expressionless except for the look in his heavy-lidded eyes. But it was a look that made me glad that I had dimmed my freckles with liquid makeup, colored my lips carefully, and worn my most expensive garment, a turtleneck sweater dress of pale green cashmere. In fact, for just a moment I forgot that I had come here not in hope of seeing that look in Mike Baker's eyes, but to hear what he had learned from the Immigration people.

When he had seated me opposite him at the round table with its red-and-white-checked cloth, I asked, "Well?"

"She landed at Heathrow nine days ago."

So at least, in all probability, she and I were on the same side of the Atlantic. "You have no idea where—"

"No. There couldn't be any record of where she went after she got through customs."

I turned my head and looked out through small thick panes of ancient window glass at the Thames, its shiny blackness reflecting lights set along the opposite bank. During my less than forty hours in London I had been too weighted with anxiety to give much thought to the city in which I found myself. But now I began to feel a sense of its oldness, its vastness, its bewildering variety, from fragments of the old Roman Wall—surely not too far from this warehouse—to fashionable discos in Mayfair. I had read about all those things, but seen none of them. Had Betsy? In God's name, where was she right now, and with whom?

A waiter took our order for steak-and-kidney pie, with ale for Michael and beer for me. When the waiter had gone Mike said, "Did you have any trouble getting here?"

"None at all." In fact, I had found the London subway a pleasant surprise. True, those stations were disquietingly deep in the earth, but there were escalators to carry you down to them and back up to the surface. And although the maps at each station gave evidence of the vastness of the underground network, one's own course of travel was traced in a distinctive color, unmarred by graffiti.

Michael held the jar of breadsticks out to me and then

took one himself. "Now it's up to you," he said. "If you don't want to tell me about your sister, I won't ask you another question. But if you want me to try to help you— well, I don't see how I can, knowing nothing but her name."

I hesitated only momentarily. True, I didn't know any-thing about *him* except his name, and that he worked for one of the more sensational London newspapers, and that he disliked resembling a popular actor. But certainly he had been helpful so far. And besides, whom else could I turn to?

While we ate the hearty food placed before us, and the ancient building shuddered now and then as the river washed around its pilings, I told him of that dream my sister and I had cherished since I was in grammar school and she was a toddler. I told of the years when, with no one but each other, we had given up the idea of college for me and a dancer's career for Betsy.

"When our aunt left us the apartment and that money, it seemed to me that nothing could stop my sister from becoming a ballerina. Sometimes I think she was driven less by her own ambition than by my ambition for her. I didn't realize it. I just thought I was expressing my love and my pride. But maybe as long as she could remember I'd made her feel that she *had* to succeed. And so finally, in desperation, she blew all that money. . . ."

I told him about that ghastly production of *Oklahoma!* "Right after that she disappeared. Then that card from her came, saying that she was in London . . ."

My voice trailed off. Mike asked, "What made you think you might find her in Soho?"

I told him about our cousin Colin Bracely, and of what his own mother had said about him in that note she had left for me. I mentioned the photograph she had saved, although perhaps toward the end of her life she had forgotten she still had it. "Here it is," I said, taking it from my shoulder bag.

He looked at the snapshot, turned it over and read the words on the reverse side, looked at the picture again.

"Café Ambroscadero, isn't it?"

"Yes, and Colin does own it, or at least manages it." I told him about my conversation with the young doorman in the too-large uniform, and then my uneasy moments in that upstairs hall. I asked, "Have you ever heard of Colin Bracely?"

"No, and I've never been in that café. But I've heard the food is rather poor, especially compared to that of other Soho restaurants. In fact—"

He broke off. I said, "In fact?"

"It's the way it is in the States. Some enterprises, including restaurants, aren't even meant to make money. They're fronts, set up to launder money made in less legitimate ways. But Jenny, why is it that you think Colin Bracely could have had anything to do with your sister coming to London?"

"They saw each other in New York a few times." I told him about running across Betsy and Colin at that sidewalk café. I told him, too, of Antonio Braselmo's joining us. "Colin said he was staying in Braselmo's apartment."

At the name Braselmo, Mike Baker's eyes had widened a little. Now he said, "Forty-odd, olive complexion, expensive tailoring?"

I nodded, my heartbeats quickening. "You know him?"

"We've never been introduced, but I know who he is. Not a nice boy. Makes money any way he can, and I mean *any* way. If your cousin is mixed up with him, then your aunt must have been right about her son." He paused. "But why on earth do you think that either of those two men would have induced your sister to come to London?"

"Why—why, for one thing, there's her looks. See for yourself." I took out my billfold with its plastic compartments for my father's photograph and my mother's and Betsy's, and handed it to him.

As he studied it I said, "It doesn't show up in the snapshot, but there's a little fleck of green in her right eye. People say it makes her even more attractive."

He handed the billfold back to me. "She's a very pretty girl, all right, especially if your taste runs to blond ingenue types."

I gained the impression that he meant his taste did not. I felt a little ashamed of the pleasure brought me by the thought that perhaps he preferred girls with russet hair, despite the freckles that so often go with it.

"But Jenny, there are many, many pretty eighteen-year-old blondes. Unless your cousin or this Braselmo fellow fell deeply in love—and it's hard to imagine men like that being in love—neither of them would have gone to the trouble and expense of transporting your sister across the Atlantic."

I turned my beer glass in a circle on the table, wanting to believe his words and yet not convinced by them. "But how did she get here, then? She had no money. She'd given it all to that theatrical group."

"Are you sure of that? Sure that she didn't hold back a thousand or so?"

I wasn't sure. Our financial arrangements had been of the simplest. As long as Betsy was not earning money, I was to pay our joint household expenses. She was to buy her own clothes and cosmetics out of the interest the bank paid on her behalf of the sixty thousand, plus a little of the principal, if need be. How much if anything remained in her account after her theatrical investment, I did not know.

"Besides," he was saying, "she was at least on the fringes of show business. Some of those people practically commute back and forth across the Atlantic. One of them might have staked her to the money and offered her a place to stay here.

"Now, this is what I think you should do, Jenny. Put a personal ad in the paper."

I nodded. "The policeman I talked to this morning suggested that."

"Make it the *Times*. That's still the paper most foreigners read. If she doesn't see it herself, someone may draw her attention to it. I'd run it for three days. I can put it in for you tomorrow morning."

"Shall I give the phone number of where I'm staying?"

"In the ad? No. A lot of weirdos would be calling you."

We decided upon the simplest of messages—"Betsy, write to me. I am in London. Jenny"—followed by a box number. Then Michael asked, "Have you seen much of London so far?"

"Almost nothing. I got here only yesterday morning." I thought of how, gritty-eyed after a sleepless night on the plane, I had ridden on the airport bus past miles and miles of houses—some cramped-looking semidetached villas resembling those tapestry-brick structures in Queens, others handsome Georgian houses—and finally arrived at the airport terminal in Victoria Station.

"How did you hear of Ebury Street?"

"A stewardess on the plane mentioned it. She said it was inexpensive, and close to Victoria Station. I just walked up Ebury and climbed the steps of the first house I saw with a bed-sitting room sign in the window."

"No sight-seeing yesterday?"

"No. As soon as I'd rented the room I went back to the cable office at Victoria Station and sent a cable to my apartment-house superintendent in Queens, giving him my address over here and the number of the pay phone in the hall outside my room. You see, if—if there should be a letter or any other sort of message from my sister, I want to know about it right away."

Michael nodded.

"After that I just came back to my room and fell into bed and slept and slept. I didn't wake up until almost sunset. Then I went out into the hall and opened the phone book to the advertising pages and tried to look up my cousin's restaurant."

"Tried to? Oh, yes. You told me that in the snapshot only the first three letters of the restaurant's name showed on its sign."

"That's right. There were two listed restaurants whose names began with AMB. One was on Pickney Street. Café Ambrosia, I think its name was. The other was the Ambroscadero, on Malta Street."

"How did you know which was the right one?"

"Mrs. Ryan, my landlady." She had come toiling up

the stairs while I stood there with the opened phone book in my hands. "She told me that Pickney Street is practically out in the country. It was near Hampton Court Palace, she said, where 'old Henry the Eighth used to keep his wives until he cut their heads off.' That snapshot of Colin's hadn't given me the impression that his restaurant was in the country, so I decided it must be the Malta Street one."

"Did she tell you Malta Street was in Soho?"

I nodded.

"I'll bet she warned you against going there alone."

"Did she ever!"

"Did you tell her your reason for wanting to go?"

"Lord, no. I got the feeling that Mrs. Ryan is a woman with a big heart and a curiosity to match. I think if she had any inkling of my troubles she would never rest until she learned the last details. So I just said I'd promised to look up a 'friend of a friend' who managed the Ambroscadero or a café of a similar name."

"She let you go then?"

"Scarcely. Instead she asked me down to her kitchen for tea. I thought she meant a cup of tea, so I said yes."

He smiled. "I'll bet it turned out to be what we call high tea."

"Very, very high. Buttered bread, ham, potato salad, sliced tomatoes, and raisin cake. And tea, of course. All through the meal she talked of how wicked London had become, what with pictures of naked women in nightclub windows, and policemen having to carry guns, and so on and so on. I managed to escape, finally, by telling her I'd changed my mind about going to that café. I said I'd phone

64

the friend of a friend the next day and arrange to meet him elsewhere.

"Once outside the house I consulted the transportation guide I had taken from a rack at Victoria Station that morning. Then I boarded a bus, rode up to Piccadilly Circus, and walked up that sloping street through the crowd of heavily painted women and searching-eyed men and prosperous-looking restaurantgoers.

"And so I haven't had a chance to see any of the things I've heard about. Oh, I've caught a couple of glimpses of Westminster Abbey, and I saw the Eros statue in Piccadilly Circus last night, but that's about all."

"Would you let me show you London? I have a car, a four-speed Land-Rover, although I keep it in the garage most of the time. And I have the day off tomorrow."

"That sounds—I'd like that."

"Where would you like to go first?"

"Kew Gardens, I think. I've liked that poem almost as long as I can remember."

He smiled. "I think you'll like Kew, even if it isn't lilac time."

We left the pub soon after that. Because the late-afternoon mist had lifted and the night was brilliantly clear, we decided to ride the top deck of a bus past the storied bridges—Blackfairs and Waterloo and Westminster—as they arched, brilliantly lighted, above the dark river.

When we reached Mrs. Ryan's house Michael walked up to the door with me. Since it was not yet eleven, the door had not been locked. He swung it back. In the light from the foyer, I saw a question in those heavy-lidded eyes. I let my answer, a friendly negative, show in my own eyes. I liked him a lot, but not that much, or at least not that soon.

"Good night," I said, "and thanks very much for everything."

He smiled. "See you at ten tomorrow." He cupped my chin with one hand, kissed my lips lightly, and went down the steps.

SEVEN

The paths were narrow, winding, and in some spots so overgrown that brambles tore at the legs of our jeans. Dead limbs projected from both evergreens and deciduous trees. In some places boughs mingled overhead so thickly that already, with sunset almost two hours away, we seemed to move through twilight.

It was hard to realize that we were still within the limits of Greater London. Only an occasional sign attached to a tree trunk, warning the visitor to watch out for falling branches, indicated that we were in a public park rather than some remote forest.

Michael had picked me up at eleven in his Land-Rover, a sturdy vehicle that, he told me, he used chiefly for rock-climbing expeditions in the Midlands and Scotland. We had driven up to an area called Knightsbridge, where a broad avenue was bordered by expensive-looking stores. I had heard of one of them, Harrods. We drove past another landmark I had heard of, Albert Hall. Across from it was the pile of masonry depicted on that postcard Betsy had sent me. It was Queen Victoria's memorial to her husband, Mike said, and it was probably at once the ugliest and most fascinating monument in the world, teeming with elephants, lions, Greek philosophers, medieval churchmen, and nineteenth-century scientists, all gathered to pay homage to the grieving widow's Prince Albert.

"It's like a huge cake concocted by a totally insane baker," Mike said. "We'll have to take a closer look at it sometime soon."

Despite that enigmatic postcard in my purse, despite the anxiety that was never far from my consciousness, I felt my spirits lift at the prospect of a future visit to the Albert Memorial or anything else with Mike.

"By the way," he said, "I put your personal in the *Times*. It will be in tomorrow's edition and for two additional days. I've got the receipt with the box number in my wallet. Remind me to give it to you."

"I will."

We drove on past the dark red brick mass of Kensington Palace, where, Mike said, Princess Margaret and her offspring lived. Soon the neighborhood began to change to something resembling Manhattan's upper Broadway. Music stores blared rock from open doorways, and sidewalk stalls offered sneakers and T-shirts. This, Mike said, was Hammersmith. Then the area became more suburban, with semidetached villas and, occasionally, a sizable house set back behind tall hedges. And then we had reached the Royal Garden at Kew.

Before entering the gate in the high wall, we bought a box lunch from a little tearoom a few hundred yards away. Then we left the Land-Rover in the car park, bought our tickets at the gate, and walked along a graveled path to the river's edge. There we sat on a bench, ate our lunch, and looked across the sun-dazzled Thames at a stone mansion with a large bronze lion on its roof. The lion, Mike said, was part of the coat of arms of the noble lord who had built the place. He had a falling out with Queen Victoria and, to make his feelings clear, turned the lion around so that its tail pointed toward Buckingham Palace.

I laughed and then said, "You love London, don't you?"

He nodded. "I love the whole country. Oh, I know that today we've got about as much international clout as Liechtenstein does. I suppose that to some it's downright laughable to see the Horse Guards parading in their the-sun-never-sets bearskins and swords and gold braid. And of course there's the crime getting out of hand, and the racial clashes, and the unemployment. But if the old island had gone twice as far downhill, I'd still love it, if only for its history. Queen Boadicea setting the Roman Legions back on their heels, and bonfires blazing from one end of England to the other while the Armada's wreckage washed ashore, and Churchill snarling that we'd fight them on the beaches and in the hills, that we'd never surrender. . . ."

His voice trailed off. I said, "You were born in London weren't you?"

"That's right. Within sound of Bow Bells." He gave me a sidelong smile. "Did you guess that?" When I nodded he said, "How?"

"British TV shows we see in America. Lots of them have Cockney characters."

He told me then that his father, a bookkeeper, had been unable to afford to send him to the sort of private establishment known in England as a public school. However, he had gone to Cambridge on a partial scholarship.

"Then why—"

I checked myself, but he had guessed what I was about to say. "Then why, with a university education, didn't I go to work for the *Times* or the *Economist* instead of one of the more sensational sheets? Well, I don't agree with the *Economist*'s politics and I do like my paper's, regrettable as I may find its taste in other respects. And it pays well. That's important to me.

"Oh, not that I'm aiming for tycoonship and a knighthood," he went on. "But I would like to accumulate enough so that I could spend a couple of years traveling around the world, visiting all of the railways that still use steam."

"Steam! You mean steam locomotives?"

He nodded. "They've been an enthusiasm of mine for almost as long as I can remember. If possible, I'd like to write a series of articles or even books about steam trains in China and India, and the few that are left in Europe. I can't imagine a better life than traveling around the world and getting paid for it."

When we had finished our lunch we went to nearby Kew Palace, which Mike said was the smallest royal residence in Britain. As a matter of fact, it looked more like a prosperous farmhouse than a palace. We looked though rooms where poor George the Third had lived while losing his wits and the American colonies, and where Victoria was born, and where George the Fourth had lived for a while with that wild creature, Queen Caroline, who ran off finally to join a European circus and ride bare-breasted in parades through Italian cities.

After we left the palace we wandered past flower beds where, even though it was almost October, annuals of every sort, as well as dahlias and gladiolas and early chrysanthemums, bloomed riotously. We visited a vast greenhouse where orchids and giant ferns flourished in the warm moist air. And then, at Mike's suggestion, we went deeper into the park to the area that deliberately had been left in a state of nature, its tree branches untrimmed, its hollow limbs left to provide homes for owls and woodpeckers. At last we came to a little tarn, dank-smelling, its surface overgrown with some sort of dark green vegetation. As we stood there in the fading light, I thought of how different this place was from Central Park, say. Evidently we had penetrated to an area where few people came. In fact, we had seen only two persons, both middle-aged women, in the past twenty minutes or so, although we had heard the voices of people on other paths. It would be foolhardy individuals indeed who would visit an area this lonely in Central Park. And yet here I had no sense of lurking threat, nor did Michael seem to.

"We'd better start back," he said. "This place closes at dusk."

We turned back along a path so narrow that we moved single file through the gloom beneath the thickly mingled branches. We walked fifty feet, perhaps seventy-five. Then there was a crackling sound and a stirring of the air close to my face. Michael, walking ahead of me, halted so abruptly that I ran into him. Whirling around, he seized my upper arms and dragged me down with him into the underbrush. Again I heard a cracking noise.

Somewhere up the path a woman said, "What was that?" A man answered, "It sounded like shots."

Other noises now, off somewhere to the right. Crackle of underbrush, thud of retreating footsteps. Then Michael was lifting me, dazed, to my feet.

People were coming around a bend in the path. A stout middle-aged man, a thin boy of about fourteen, and a middle-aged woman, also plump. The man said, "What's the trouble here?"

Pulling a twig free from his denim jacket, Mike said grimly, "Someone took a couple of shots at us."

The young boy said, "Crikey!" and his mother wailed, "I don't know what in heaven's name this country is—"

"We'd better get away from here," Michael said. "All of us."

Moving ahead of Michael now, dimly aware of disheveled clothing and hair and a scratch on my cheek, I followed the couple and their son along the path. Soon the part of the garden set aside for untended woodland gave way to cultivated areas of grassy knolls and extensive flower beds. The day seemed to grow earlier, now that branches no longer cut off the past-sunset light. The paths were wider and filled with people moving toward the exit.

When we had gone through the gates with the couple and their son, Mike said, "We're going to report this to the police, of course. May I give them your names as witnesses?"

The boy looked pleasurably excited. His parents looked

glumly resigned to doing their duty. It turned out that they were Albert Madden, his wife Helen, and their son, Albert Junior. We thanked them, said good-bye, and walked to the Land-Rover in the car park.

Michael said, "There's a police station beyond that tea shop where we bought our lunch."

EIGHT

In the car I tried to repair some of the damage to my appearance, combing my hair and wiping dirt and a little blood from my face and picking twigs from my green turtleneck and jeans. Nevertheless, when we entered the small police station I saw speculation leap into the eyes of the uniformed man behind the desk. Plainly he wondered whether I was drunk, or a rape victim, or an accident survivor.

"We want to report an assault," Michael said. "Someone fired a gun at us."

In a small side room, a Sergeant Rusher, a graying man with nicotine-stained fingers, took our statement. "What sort of firearm did it sound like? A rifle?"

"I'd say so," Mike answered.

"Perhaps it was an air rifle. Thick woods like those can distort a sound and make it seem louder."

"An air rifle!"

"Yes. Young boys have been hunting rabbits and squirrels in the wilder parts of the park lately. Filthy little brutes. How they smuggle the rifles past the gate we haven't found out. Possibly they just toss them over the wall in some remote spot and then go inside through the gate and pick them up."

Michael's expression was grim. "I don't think it was an air rifle."

Sergeant Rusher's gaze grew more intent. "Do you have reason to think someone might try to harm you?"

Mike hesitated. I said, "If someone fired at us, it was probably because of me."

"You, miss?"

I told him about my sister's disappearance, and the postcard from London, and my own flight across the Atlantic. I saw the interest fade from his eyes. Like that other policeman in the station near Mrs. Ryan's place, he began to look bored and a little annoyed.

"But why should someone take a shot at you because your sister flew to London?"

"Don't you see? If she were kidnapped, or under some other form of duress—"

"Did her postcard say anything about being kidnapped?"

"No, but—" In mute appeal I looked at Michael. What I saw in that heavy-lidded face heartened me. Last night he had appeared almost as skeptical as this policeman. He didn't appear so now.

"Whatever the reason," he said to Sergeant Rusher, "someone shot at Miss Carr, or at me, or at both of us."

"Very well. We'll investigate. We'll interview that Madden couple and their son as to what they heard. And we'll try to find the bullets. But it won't be easy, whether they are steel-jacketed or just air rifle pellets. I know that area of Kew. Lots of underbrush. Lots of dead branches a bullet could penetrate into and hide. And there's a pool in there with about two feet of mud on the bottom. You could search for weeks and not find a bullet, even if it's there. But we'll look."

He pushed back his chair. "Would you like to show me the exact spot, Mr. Baker, so that we can start searching there in the morning? Perhaps Miss Carr would rather wait here for us."

It was dark by the time Michael returned to the police station with Sergeant Rusher, and well past nine by the time the Land-Rover stopped in front of Mrs. Ryan's. We'd had dinner on the way home, if you could call it that. Because I did not want to appear, disheveled as I was, in a public place, Michael had stopped at a restaurant in Chiswick, gone inside, and emerged with two boxes of fish and chips.

When we entered Mrs. Ryan's house Michael seemed to assume he could accompany me to my bed-sitter. I did not object. When I had unlocked my door, I told him to go inside. Then I went down the hall to the bathroom, where I combed my hair and bathed the scratch on my cheek.

In the tiny foyer of my room, Michael stood inspecting a print of Rossetti's "The Three Graces" on the wall. Face grim, he turned around as I entered. "All right. Let's talk."

We sat facing each other from opposite ends of a settee upholstered in some well-worn tapestrylike fabric. "Jenny, I want you to go home."

I said, bewildered, "Home!"

"Go back to New York."

"Go back! Are you crazy? With Betsy still missing some-where here in—"

"You don't know that she's still here. She may have gone back to New York herself." Then, as if he realized that was weak, he added quickly, "Those shots today may have had nothing to do with your sister. It may have been, just as that sergeant said, some delinquent with an air rifle. But let's suppose that wasn't the case. Let's suppose they were real bullets, and aimed at you. Don't you see that means you're in terrible danger?"

I saw it, of course. An awareness that someone might have been trying to kill me had lain like something cold in the pit of my stomach for the last two hours. I said, "Maybe someone's just—just trying to frighten me into going home."

"Then let him frighten you. The next time, whether intentionally or unintentionally, he might hit you."

"But if I'm careful not to go to isolated places like—"

"You can't be careful twenty-four hours a day."

"But now that the police—"

"The police aren't going to do a damn thing about it. Why should they? Unless they find a bullet or two in those woods, and the chances are overwhelming that they will not, they'll have no evidence that a crime of any sort has been committed—unless you call hunting rabbits with an air rifle a crime.

"Now go back to New York. If your sister writes to that *Times* box number, I'll be the one to pick up the letter, and find out from her what this is all about."

"No! Betsy is the only family I've got. Now that I know for sure that she came to England, do you think I'm going to turn tail and—"

78

"You damned little fool! Do you think that you're going to do your sister any good by getting yourself killed?"

Through my bewilderment and fear, a sudden rage boiled up. "Maybe the truth is that *you're* scared. You'd like to be rid of me. Is that why you want me to leave London?"

I saw that his face had flushed, and then gone white. Nevertheless, I rushed on. "Oh, it's understandable. Why should you get yourself shot at because of a girl you scarcely know? Well, that's all right. Go on. Forget you ever met me."

After a long moment he said, "You sure know how to get rid of a chap in a hurry, don't you?"

Getting to his feet, he took out his wallet, extracted a slip of blue paper, and laid in on the rickety little table at one end of the settee. Then he walked out into the hall and closed the door behind him. I heard his footsteps on the stairs. Then, a few moments later, I heard the Land-Rover's engine start.

What, I wondered numbly, had made me say that, almost the worst thing I could have said to him? Had it been the accumulated nerve strain of many days, or the lingering terror of that moment when some sort of missile had hurtled past my face, or my bewilderment now as to what course I should follow? Perhaps it had been a combination of those factors. Whatever the reason, I had alienated a man who had become very important to me in more ways than one.

I reached for the slip of paper he had left. It was a receipt from the *Times* giving the box number of the ad he had placed for me in the personal column.

NINE

I lay awake for a long time that night. Even after Big Ben struck twelve reverberating notes, I kept thinking that I might hear the Land-Rover stop beneath my window, and then a light tap on the downstairs door. Even after I gave up that notion, I still lay wondering how I could have let my nerves, no matter how overstrained, get so disastrously out of hand.

Dawn must have been close when I finally fell asleep. Consequently I awoke to flooding sunlight. I lifted my watch from the bedside stand. Almost eleven.

The *Times* would have been on sale for hours by now.

I swung out of bed, took a quick shower in that huge old tub down the hall, returned to my room to dress. Without seeing Mrs. Ryan or anyone else, I went down the stairs and out onto the sidewalk. Turning left, I hurried to the newsstand where the same stout old woman, still in those cheerful red stockings, sat in her wooden chair. I greeted her, bought the *Times*, and, still standing there, looked through it for the personal columns.

My ad was there all right: "Betsy, write to me. I am in London. Jenny." A box number followed.

"Hello, Jenny."

For one wonderful instant, until I realized the voice wasn't his, I thought Mike had come up behind me. I turned. My cousin Colin stood there, dapper in gray flannels and a darker gray cashmere sweater over a pink cotton shirt.

He said, smiling, "Caught up with you, didn't I?"

With my hands automatically refolding the newspaper, I looked at the dark wavy hair gleaming in the sunlight and the still handsome, although puffy, face.

"How did you—"

"How did I know where to look for you? I'm going to make you play twenty questions to get the answer to that. The pubs should be open by now, and there's a nice one just down the street."

"No, wait! I need to know this instant. Can you tell me where Betsy is?"

"Betsy? Did she come with you to London?"

My gaze searched that bland face. He said, "Come on. I can see we'd better talk."

I walked with him to the pub. The saloon bar with its cozy red-flocked wallpaper and gilt-framed mirrors and little round tables was already filling with people I judged to be neighborhood office workers. A waitress brought beer to Colin and a pot of tea and what she called a sweet bun to me.

He said, "So that's why you came to my restaurant the other night. You thought I might know something about Betsy."

"The doorman told you I'd been there?"

"Yes. From his description I was sure it was you."

Had that been how he knew? Or had it been valid, that feeling that had assailed me in the newly varnished hall, that sense that he was looking at me through the door's mirrored peephole?

"But how did you track me to this neighborhood?"

"Ah! That's where the twenty-question part comes in. Now where did you first hear of Ebury Street?"

"On the plane. The stewardess told me that if I wanted a place to stay that was inexpensive and centrally located—"

"Maybe she did say that. But that wasn't the first time you heard of Ebury Street. Now think!"

"Colin, I'm in no mood to play games."

"All right, all right! Remember that day you joined Betsy and me at that sidewalk café on Columbus Avenue? Later on Tony Braselmo happened by. Anyway, the talk turned to English hotels, and I mentioned that when I first visited London—my old man gave me the trip for finishing my freshman year at college—I stayed in a bed-sitter on Ebury Street."

I had no memory of his saying that. But I had been so upset that day by the discovery that my young sister associated with men like Colin and Braselmo that I probably missed some of what was said.

"I was out of town when you came to the restaurant the other night," Colin was saying. "But when I heard about it I figured you might very well be staying in one of the houses along here. Anyway, it seemed worth the short trip."

Was that how he had found me, just through a lucky

guess? It was possible, I supposed. But it seemed to me more likely that he had been not "out of town" but standing behind that peephole three nights earlier. As soon as I turned away from his door, he could have told someone to follow me. Perhaps the "someone" had been with him in his flat. Perhaps he had phoned to some hanger-on of his downstairs in the restaurant. Anyway, probably I was trailed as I walked back through Soho and encountered those two creeps, and then, after saying good night to Mike Baker, took the bus to Ebury Street.

And two days later, I now felt almost certain, Mike and I had been trailed as we drove to Kew and then walked deep into that tangle of underbrush and untrimmed trees. Again, he must have given the assignment to someone else. It was hard for me to picture my impeccably dressed and somewhat out of condition cousin firing from an ambush of dead limbs and brambles.

Colin said, "Now what's all this about Betsy?"

"She flew from New York to London about two weeks ago. I didn't know that, though, until I got a postcard from her last Thursday."

"Did her card give you an address?"

"No. That's why I came to see you."

"You thought I might know where she was?"

"It seemed possible. After all, she had known you were in business in London."

"Incidentally, I don't recall telling you the name of my café. What's more, my private phone isn't listed. So how—"

"I found a snapshot in your mother's apartment. It showed you standing beside a car in front of your restaurant."

"Ah, yes. I remember. Every once in a while I'd give way to a temptation to demonstrate that you didn't have to wear a monkey suit at West Point to get somewhere in the world." He paused, his lip curling slightly, and then went on, "But Betsy never phoned me, although I think I do recall giving her my London number once. My hunch, Jenny, is that she came over here with someone her own age, or maybe a group of kids. After all, there were friends of hers you didn't know, weren't there?"

I nodded.

"Tell me, did you and she have some kind of row before she split?"

I hesitated, and then decided to tell him. After all, there was a chance that he was as ignorant about my troubles and Betsy's as he appeared to be.

When I finished telling him about the thirty thousand, he said, "Wow! No wonder the kid wanted to run and hide. Well, you'll find her, sooner or later. It might be sooner if you put a personal in the *Times*, say."

"I already have."

I unfolded the paper to the personal columns and placed it flat on the table in front of him. I saw his gaze go straight to the bottom of the last column of newsprint, where my ad appeared. Then he looked at me and asked, "Where is your ad?"

A small thing, but enough to make every nerve in my body tighten. He had been telling an implicit lie when he pretended not to know that I had already placed an ad in the *Times*. And that meant that in all probability he was lying about everything else.

There in that cozy room, surrounded by laughing, chattering clerks and stenographers, I was suddenly sure beyond any doubt that he had caused those shots to be fired at Michael Baker and me. Perhaps the purpose had been just to frighten us, but he'd done it.

And I also felt a cold certainty that he knew where my young sister was.

I leaned across the table, touched the ad with my fingertips. "There it is."

"So it is." He refolded the paper and placed it beside my plate. "Well, that should do it. You'll hear from her."

Gaze steady on his face, I asked abruptly, "Is Mr. Braselmo in London?"

If he betrayed himself this time, my eye didn't catch it. All I saw in his face was surprise. "Tony? Why, not that I know of. The last time I heard, he was in the Bahamas somewhere." He gave a sudden laugh. "You don't think he has anything to do with your little sister running off, do you?"

My voice was cool. "I thought it possible."

"Tony? No way."

"Why? Is he gay?"

"No. Far from it. But staying well supplied with attractive women is no problem for him. He'd never involve himself with some kid running away from a mess she's made. Now, don't worry about her. It'll turn out okay."

I didn't answer. I was thinking of that corridor on the floor above the restaurant, and of that door with the mirrored peephole. It had a Yale-type lock. It would be almost impossible for someone with no expertise to get past that lock. But the corridor had stretched backward toward the stairs at the building's rear—

"What are you doing this evening?"

86

My nerves grew even tauter. "Nothing in particular. Why?"

"I'm going to see this man outside of London, in Essex. He's going to open a gambling club there, and he wants to talk to me about catering for the place. If you wanted to call a cab and join us for dinner around nine o'clock, we'll have finished our business by then. I think you'd enjoy seeing the place. It's not exactly a stately home, but it's pretty impressive. It'll be a longish cab ride. I'll pay for it when you get there."

I pictured a big country house at the end of a long drive. I thought of leaving the cab and going up steps through the darkness into the house—and not coming out.

No, it was most unlikely that he had any such intentions. If he had been responsible for those shots fired in Kew Gardens, then of course he was aware that we must have gone to the police. True, the police seemed unlikely to do anything more about those shots. But if, only thirty-six or forty-eight hours later, Mrs. Ryan reported that her American guest, Miss Jennifer Carr, had disappeared . . .

He wouldn't run the risk of a serious police investigation concerning me, not unless it became absolutely necessary. Probably what he had in mind for tonight was just an attempt to learn more about what I knew or had guessed, and to allay my suspicion further.

Or, if I was completely wrong about him—and that was possible—then all he might have in mind was entertaining his American cousin at no more cost than that of a taxi fare.

But the nature of his plans for that evening didn't really matter because—despite the fact that I was nodding assent—I had no intention of being a part of those plans.

"That sounds interesting," I said.

"I'll write down what you're to tell the cabbie."

He drew a pencil and notebook from the pocket of his gray flannels, ripped out a page, and began to write. When he'd handed the page to me, he asked, "What's the phone number where you're staying?"

I told him.

TEN

We parted soon after that. He had an appointment, he said, with some restaurant-supply wholesalers at one o'clock. As for me, guided by the street map I had bought at Victoria Station the morning of my arrival in London, I made my way to the *Times* building on Fleet Street. No one had handed in a reply to my advertisement, and of course it was too early for an answer to have arrived through the mail.

As I walked back to the bus stop I came to a shop with a sign above the door that read simply: "Harper's." From the contents of its windows, though—garden hose and kitchen step stools and small appliances—I knew it must be a hardware store. Inside I bought a skeleton key. True, it wouldn't unlock Colin's front door, but it might open some other one.

When I returned to Mrs. Ryan's I looked up the number of that police substation near Kew Gardens and dialed it. No, Sergeant Rusher told me, a search of that area of the park had revealed no bullets, nor bullet scars on tree trunks or branches. I returned to my room and, sitting beside the window, tried to concentrate on the paperback copy of Michener's *Chesapeake* that I had bought at the airport in New York.

Four times during that long afternoon the wall phone out in the hall rang. Each time I hurried to it, heartbeats rapid with the hope that it was Michael, or the apartment-house superintendent back in Queens saying he had word of Betsy. Or, by some wild chance, Betsy herself. Once the caller hung up as soon as I spoke. Another time someone was trying to reach a chemist's shop. The other times a man called for "Miss Florence Smythe, in the first floor rear." Knowing that by "first" he meant what Americans call second, I walked back along the hall to Miss Smythe's door. Both times I had to report to him that she did not answer my knock.

At seven o'clock, dressed in jeans and a gray sweat shirt and sneakers, I left the house. Once again I took the bus to Piccadilly Circus and then, nerves strung tight, walked up that sloping street through the sidewalk crowd of sightseers, booted-and-miniskirted girls, and men with appraising eyes.

As I approached the Café Ambroscadero I saw that it had a new doorman. This one also was too small for his uniform. A round-shouldered man with grayish red hair hanging beneath his cap in back, he stood chatting with a cabdriver who had parked at the curb. I turned and darted inside that doorway beside the restaurant, too weighted with my own anxiety to feel more than fleeting guilt at the thought that the young Indian might have been fired on my account.

I went up the stairs swiftly, aware that by doing so I made the stairs creak, but feeling it was best to get in and out of the place as quickly as possible. At the head of the stairs I looked to my left, where the varnished door of Colin's flat gleamed harshly in the overhead light. No sounds except distant voices and the honk of horns filtering up the stairs from the street.

I turned and hurried to the flight of stairs at the rear end of the hall. There, the carpeting was older than that of the front stairs. The door at the bottom was a heavy steel one, bolted. I tugged at the bolt, praying that the door was not locked as well. It was not. When the bolt finally slid back it was easy to swing the door open. I stepped out into the last of the daylight and closed the door behind me.

I found myself in a barren yard, separated from what was apparently an alley by a high wooden fence. A door in the fence was secured by a wooden bolt. I stood flattened against the building's brick wall and looked to my left. A few feet away a metal staircase led upward. Beyond the foot of the stairs was a door similar to the one through which I had just emerged. Beyond the second door, broad windows set at ground level spilled light and the clatter of dishes and the voices of men speaking some foreign language out into the yard. The restaurant's kitchen.

I looked at the metal staircase again. It led up the rear wall to a small platform and a door. The chances were overwhelming that, like the door at ground level, it was bolted from the inside. But it had an upper pane of frosted glass—

Swiftly I looked around me. Near my feet was a strip of metal that looked like a badly rusted tire iron. Praying that no aproned cook, wanting a breath of air, would step out into the yard and look upward, I climbed to the platform. I'd drawn my arm back, ready to try to shatter that glass pane as swiftly and quietly as possible, when it occurred to me that perhaps—

I tried the door's metal knob. It turned under my hand, and the door swung back.

I laid the tire iron quietly on the platform, unwilling to drop it into the yard lest it strike with a clang against some other bit of metal. Then I stepped through the door and closed it silently behind me.

Enough light came through the frosted pane to show me that I was in a room about twenty feet square, with barrels and crates set on its bare floor. Opposite me was another door. I crossed to it, tried the knob. Not so lucky this time. The knob didn't turn. But beneath it I could feel an old-fashioned keyhole.

I'd never thought of myself as psychic. But as I carefully inserted that newly purchased skeleton key, and heard the lock turn, I felt that some sort of premonition had guided me into that hardware store a few hours earlier.

I swung the door back as noiselessly as possible, restored the key to the pocket of my jeans, closed the door behind me. I was in a narrow carpeted hallway, with an open doorway at its end framing near-darkness. For several seconds I stood motionless, heart hammering with the thought that at any moment a figure—Colin's? someone else's?—might blot out the faint light at the other end of the hall.

No one appeared, and I heard no sounds except distant ones from the street. After a while I moved forward along the hall. To my right there was a partially opened door. I halted, held my breath, and gave the door a slight push. The room was a small bedroom, with gray twilight filtering through venetian blinds onto a chest of drawers and a neatly made bed.

A few steps farther down the hall was a bathroom, its door also partially opened. Then I entered the flat's main room. Only a glimmer of daylight came through the windows overlooking the street. If I was to accomplish anything by this stealthy visit, I would have to have light. I stood motionless for a moment, aware of the sound of my own blood in my ears, and then reached out to the wall beside me. After a moment my groping fingers found a switch.

Light from a brass ceiling fixture blazed down on green wall-to-wall carpeting, a big sofa and two oversized armchairs in fake black leather, a flat-topped desk bearing a phone with an attached answering machine, a black plastic pen and pencil slanting up from a black plastic base, and an onyx clock. Near the desk was a low wooden filing cabinet. On one of the brown painted walls hung a bas relief of some silvery-looking metal. Its subject was a reclining nude. Between the two windows stood a TV set and a liquor cabinet of the sort that opens up into a bar. Evidently my cousin had all his food sent up from the restaurant, because there was no door that could have led to a kitchen.

The clock on the desk chimed nine. I thought of Colin at that country house, waiting for my taxi to draw up in front—

I moved toward the desk and the filing cabinet. If there

was anything in this flat to indicate that Colin was in some way connected with Betsy's disappearance, surely his desk was the most likely place to find it.

The top drawer first. Colin was such a dapper man that it was a surprise to find that drawer a mess. Old envelopes, bills, loose stamps, an empty cigarette wrapper, theater ticket stubs. I pawed through the drawer hastily, sure that he would keep nothing of importance here.

The side drawers were neater, but they held only boxed letter paper, carbon paper, pencils, ball-point pens, and two fresh-looking decks of playing cards.

The filing cabinet, then.

But it held only cardboard folders with labels like "Bills Outstanding," and "Taxes," and "Householding Expenses," and "Insurance." What was more, the contents of each folder seemed to fit its label.

True, there appeared to be no records relating to the restaurant business. Perhaps those books were kept in some office adjoining the restaurant itself. But anyway, if there were any evidence connecting him with Betsy, it would be here in this flat, not in some downstairs office.

Perhaps in the bedroom?

As might be expected of a man so careful of his appearance, my cousin's bureau was in good order, one drawer given over to shirts, another to sweaters and scarves, another to underwear. But clothing was all they held. The same was true of the closet, with its row of suits and jackets and its shoes arranged on a stand.

I walked back to the bureau to something I had not yet investigated, a carved wooden box beside the comb and brush set. I opened it. Nothing inside except gold chains, a pair of gold cuff links, and a wristwatch with a steel case.

Well, I thought, I should have realized as soon as I found the unlocked door at the top of those outdoor stairs that I was wasting my energy. If the flat held anything incriminating, Colin would have made it more resistant to clandestine searchers. And yet I had been so sure that I would find something here to help me. I think I'd even had a faint hope of finding Betsy herself here.

I told myself that I might as well face the fact that this could have been almost any bachelor flat, equipped with a supposedly sophisticated equivalent of a nudie wall calendar, and with a bar, and a telephone equipped with an answering machine—

That answering machine.

Swiftly I went back into the living room, picked up the phone, punched a button on the attached device.

Evidently Colin really had conferred with some restaurant-supply people early that afternoon, because someone had called and left a message about that meeting. A petulant-sounding girl who did not identify herself had called with a three-word message: "Colin! Ring me." A Mr. Cavendish in Richmond hoped to sell him a used Porsche.

And my sister had telephoned.

When I first heard her voice, light and rather breathless and definitely indignant, I was so stunned that for several seconds I could not absorb what she was saying. When the recorded message ended, I pushed a button with a shaking finger and again heard her voice.

"Now you listen to me, Colin! Whether you like it or not, I've moved. I told you I didn't like that hotel. It had *cockroaches*. I can see why Tony might not want me staying at some place like the Ritz, but I don't think he'd want me staying at a crummy place like that one, either. I'm sure he gave you money for a nice hotel, and you gave me only part of it. Anyway, I don't care if I have to cut down on other things, even food. I've left that place.

"Now I'm staying at the Hotel du Rivage, Rue de Saint Peres. That's just off the Boulevard St. Germain. I've registered under the same name. Tell Tony."

A click.

I played it once more, making sure of the name of the hotel. A Paris hotel? I was sure of it. Two women who worked at the bank in Carrsville had gone to Paris one summer and stayed in a Left Bank hotel off the Boulevard St. Germain.

There was a button on the machine marked "Total Rewind." I pressed it, hoping that it would rewind the tape so that Colin would never know that someone had listened to his messages. But even if he did know, and even if he suspected the intruder might be me, I still felt infinitely thankful that I had come here. I knew now that Betsy was alive, and that she sounded well, although ill-tempered. And I knew where she was.

The doorbell rang.

My first panicky impulse was to run. Pulses racing, I whirled around, started down that short inner hall toward the flat's rear entrance. But before I reached it the doorbell gave another ring, a short, impatient-sounding one, and then another. I realized that whoever stood out there almost surely didn't have a key. If he had, he would have used it by this time.

I wondered who it was who stood on the other side of that front door. Could it possibly be the silk-suited, balding man I'd been introduced to on Columbus Avenue one hot day? Whether it was or not, the more I knew about

Colin's associates the better. I moved back to the living room and, grateful for the wall-to-wall carpeting, walked quickly and quietly to the front door and looked through the peephole.

Not Tony Braselmo out in the hall. Someone I had never seen before, a thin-faced man in his early twenties with lank blondish hair and a barely visible scar on his upper lip. To judge by his scowl, he was very disappointed about something. He gave the doorbell another jab and then, still scowling, turned away. I heard his muffled footsteps descend the stairs.

Heartbeats less rapid now, I turned out the light and then again went down that inner hall. On the other side of the flat's rear door I turned the skeleton key in the lock, dropped the key into the pocket of my jeans. Then I crossed the storeroom. On the little platform at the head of the outdoor stairs I picked up the rusted tire iron. A few feet beyond the foot of the stairs I laid it down in the dirt and then hesitated. Should I leave the way I had come? No. Something warned me that if I went inside the building, climbed the steps to that red-carpeted corridor, and then descended to the street, I would be pushing my luck too far. For instance, that thin youth with the scowl might, for some reason or other, be lingering in the doorway to the street. Or that doorman might see me emerge, and later on tell Colin.

True, if I didn't go back into the building I couldn't rebar that door at the foot of the rear stairs. But that wasn't too important, I decided. Almost anyone, including some prankish kids sneaking into the building off the street, could have unbarred the door.

I went to the gate in the high wooden fence. It had a

97

latch-string bar, similar to the one on our backyard gate in Carrsville. I threaded the length of cord through the hole provided and then opened the gate. Out in the alley I closed the gate, used the cord to maneuver the bar into place, and then poked the string back through the hole.

The alley was empty. I walked perhaps fifty feet and then turned onto a branching alley that led toward the well-lighted street. Near the alley's mouth stood three girls, skimpy-skirted and booted, one of them brown-skinned, two of them white. They looked at me with speculative, faintly hostile eyes, but said nothing.

I hurried down the thronged sidewalk. Near the Piccadilly Circus bus stop there was a travel bureau. Even though I knew it would be closed at this time of night I went to it and looked in the window. Yes, just as I had remembered, the window held a timetable for cross-Channel travelers, giving the hours for the Le Havre boats and the train ferries to Holland and the British Airways flights to Paris, Milan, and Rome. I made a mental note of the time for the morning plane to Paris, and then went back to the bus stop.

Within minutes after I reached my room at Mrs. Ryan's the hall phone rang. Almost sure who was calling, I went out and took down the instrument. "Hello."

Colin said, "I've waited more than an hour. Why the hell aren't you here?"

"I'm sorry, so terribly sorry. I lost that piece of paper you gave me, the one with instructions for the cabbie. I had no way of letting you know . . ."

My voice trailed off. When he again spoke it was in a tone of forced good humor. "Well, it can't be helped. How about fixing something up for later on? I have to go out of town for a couple of days, but after that—"

"Thanks, Colin, but I think I may be going home about then."

"Home? You mean to Queens?"

"Yes. If I won't get an answer to my ad—well, maybe that will be because she's already back in New York. Anyway, I can't afford to stay over here, particularly after she lost half our money. My boss isn't paying me, and if I stay away much longer I wouldn't blame him for firing me."

"Too bad that you have to go back so soon." Perhaps he wasn't aware of how relieved he sounded. "But as I told you, I think you've worried unnecessarily about Betsy. She'll turn up."

He went on, "I'll say good-bye now, in case I don't see you again before you go. But we'll probably be running into each other again soon, on one side of the Atlantic or the other."

We hung up. I went into my room and packed a tote bag, so that I would have plenty of time in the morning for the bus trip to the London airport.

ELEVEN

At Heathrow a sullen drizzle had been falling onto the tarmac. It was falling now through the gray early-afternoon light as a taxi carried me down the ancient Paris street, a twisting street so narrow that cars were parked with two wheels on the sidewalk.

The cab stopped before a building of gray stone, narrow-fronted and with bulging ground-floor windows. I paid the driver, a middle-aged woman who had a part-collie dog curled on the seat beside her. (The dog was there, she explained in accented English, to scare off passengers who might try to rob her.) I went into the hotel.

Its narrow lobby was modest indeed, equipped with a sofa upholstered in well-worn brown tweed, several folding chairs with blue plastic seats and metal arms, and a TV set, its screen blank at the moment. The clerk behind the desk, an elderly man, told me that yes, there was a single room available. He opened a registration book to a blank page—apparently I was the only new guest so far that day—and then turned to inspect the rows of keys behind the desk.

Swiftly I flipped back to yesterday's page in the register. A Paul Seeger from Chicago had registered for himself and his wife. And a Georges somebody-or-other from Bordeaux had signed in the register in an almost illegible hand.

I turned to the page before that. Six guests had registered that day. The left-slanted handwriting of the last one, a "Miss Nancy Allen of Detroit," seemed to leap off the page at me.

Nancy had always been my little sister's favorite name. I had a poignant memory of her giving a dolls' tea party under the big elm in our front yard, with Nancy Sue seated on her right, and Nancy Irene on her left, and Nancy Helen, a rag doll who had lost a leg to our Dalmatian puppy, cradled in her lap.

By the time the old man turned around, a heavy key in one hand and a ball-point pen in the other, I had turned the register once more to that day's blank page. He said, "I am putting you on the fourth floor, mademoiselle."

I signed my name and then said, "I think you have a friend of mine staying here. Her name is Nancy Allen."

The way his face lighted up told me that he was not too old to appreciate my sister. "But yes. Mademoiselle Allen."

"Do you know if she is in now?"

He did not even have to look at the row of keys in order to tell me. "Mademoiselle went to her room about an hour ago. She said she had been at lunch."

"Her room number?"

"It is fifty, mademoiselle."

Even though my only luggage was my shoulder tote, the clerk rang for a porter, a hefty young woman in a blue smock who looked as if she could handle a medium-size trunk. We rode in a tiny, grill-fronted elevator to the fourth floor, where she unlocked a door, handed me the key, and at my request tugged open a window so badly stuck that I would never have been able to open it. Then she accepted my tip and left.

I threw a hasty look around the shabby but reasonably clean room. Beige carpeting, a massive old bureau of some dark wood, a single bed with a brown velour spread, and, on the bedside table, a surprisingly frivolous lamp in the form of a plaster Columbine holding up a globe with a red shade of some silkish material. I also took a quick look into the small bathroom with its plain white fixtures. Then, pulses rapid, I went out into the hall. At both ends staircases led upward. I took the nearest one.

Number fifty was the first room I came to on the fifth floor. I knocked. Betsy called, "Who is it, please?"

I knocked again.

She opened the door. I saw astonishment in the beautiful blue eyes with the green fleck, and then gladness, and then alarm so sharp that I feared she might close the door in my face and turn the key. Quickly I slid past her into the room. She closed the door and stood with her back to it.

"How on earth did you—"

"I'll tell you later. But first I want to know how you are."

"I'm fine."

She didn't appear to be. Oh, she looked extremely pretty, even in the frayed jeans and old pink shirt that had been her favorite lounging costume for the past year or so. But she was thinner and paler than before, and there was a tense look around her mouth.

"You found out from Colin where I was, didn't you?"

"In a way."

"Tony will kill him."

After a moment I said, "All right, Betsy. Sit down. Tell me what this is all about."

She stared at me for a long moment, her face sullen, and then crossed the room and sank down on the bed. I sat on the dressing-table bench. Vaguely I was aware that this room, with its light blue bedspread and matching window draperies of some satiny material, its new-looking pearl-gray carpet and its dressing table of blond wood, was much more attractive than mine. Evidently the clerk had given her the best single room in the house.

I said, trying to keep my voice calm, "By Tony, do you mean Antonio Braselmo?"

Her gaze defiant now, she gave a brief nod.

"What does he have to do with you?"

"He's going to marry me, that's what he has to do with me."

Oh, God, I thought. Eighteen. And at the moment she looked fifteen. "Betsy, you have no idea of what you're saying. The man is a good deal more than twice your age."

"What's that got to do with anything? He's attractive, very attractive."

"Attractive! From what I hear, he's a notorious crook."

"Tony has told me all about those lying stories! Businessmen are jealous of each other, just the way actors are, or athletes. Men who aren't as successful as him say things about him, but he doesn't do anything that they don't do. Why, all international businessmen bribe foreign officials. It's standard multinational procedure."

Standard multinational procedure. That wasn't my young sister talking.

I asked, "Have you been to bed with him?"

"Not that it's any of your business, but I haven't. You see, he respects me."

That was one thing I was sure he did not do. Why should a slick, middle-aged operator like Antonio Braselmo feel anything but passing lust for a girl like Betsy, a small-town girl of only average intelligence and less than average sophistication?

Above all, why on earth should he want to marry her?

I had a sense of something dark and evil moving beneath the surface of things, something that made my stomach tighten up.

I said, still trying to speak calmly, "Tell me about it, from the beginning." When she didn't answer I went on, even though I realized that my words might bring out all the stubborn defiance. "I don't think you would have done all this if that *Oklahoma!* production hadn't flopped."

She said coldly, "All right. So I wouldn't have." After a moment she added, "Since you know this much, you might as well know the rest. For quite a while before I left New York I kept running into either Colin or Tony. It was Colin who first told me Tony was in love with me. Then Tony told me so, too, and asked me to marry him."

"And what did you say?"

"At first I told him I didn't know. But after that play flopped, and I realized I'd lost all that money, I called him up and said yes."

I couldn't resist it. "You suddenly found yourself head over heels in love with him."

Angry color dyed her cheekbones. "Maybe I did. I can think of worse people to fall in love with than a good-looking multimillionaire."

I decided to try another tack. "Did you come to London alone?"

"No, with Colin."

"Colin! Did Tony know that?"

"Of course. He asked Colin to take me to London and find me a place to stay for a while. I stayed at a hotel in Kensington."

"But *why*? Why did they want you to leave New York?"

"It was because of his wife."

"Wife? Whose wife?"

"Tony's. You see, he has to get a divorce before he can marry me. And she's—she's vindictive. He says that if she knew he was in love with someone, especially a young girl, she'd never give him a divorce, not for any amount of money."

I was silent for a stunned moment. Then I said, "I still don't see—"

"She mustn't find out about Tony and me! He was afraid she would if we both stayed in New York. Not that she was there. She spends most of her time in Rome. But friends of hers come to New York frequently. So he thought it was better if we stayed apart until the divorce went through, me in London and Tony traveling around on business."

I said, after an interval, "There was another reason why you left New York, wasn't there? You knew I'd raise hell if I found out about you and him, didn't you?"

"Yes. Tony was afraid you would do anything to try to stop us, even manage to get word to his wife. But after I'd been in London a few days I airmailed you that post-card."

"Why did you?"

"I hated the thought of your worrying."

She hated the thought of my worrying. "Did you tell Colin you were going to send the postcard?"

"No, but I did tell him the day after I'd done it."

"And it was then that he suggested that you go to Paris?"

"Yes. He said he'd gotten in touch with Tony, and Tony felt Paris would be—safer, now that you knew I'd come to London. So Colin brought me over here and found me a hotel room on the Right Bank. But it was an awful place. Cockroaches! I'm sure Colin held out some of the money Tony gave him to give to me. Then I heard I could move here for only twenty francs a day more. A waitress in a café told me about this place."

She paused and then said, "You haven't told me how you found me."

I considered. How much should I tell her? Everything, I decided. It would take all of it to convince her that she must come home with me, right now.

I told her of my visit to Soho, and of my uneasy feeling there in the hall that Colin was inspecting me through the peephole in his apartment door. I told her of my trip to Kew Gardens with Mike Baker, and the shots fired at us by some hidden sniper.

Betsy's face had turned paler. "You went to the police?"

"Yes. But the last I heard they hadn't found any bullets. Anyway, they seemed sure it was kids hunting rabbits."

"Maybe it was."

"Maybe. But Colin turned up near my bed-sitter place on Ebury Street the next day, with some phony-sounding story about how he'd happened to find me. And I know he lied to me about something else. You see, I'd put an ad in the *Times*."

I told her about the personal. "Colin pretended that he'd known nothing about it, but when I handed him the paper his eyes went straight to the spot where the ad was printed. I was sure then that he'd also been lying when he said he had no idea where you were."

I went on, telling her of Colin's invitation to join him at that country house, and my own decision that instead I'd spend that time finding out anything I could in his flat.

"Oh, Jenny! You broke into his place?"

"Well, I *got* into it. It wasn't hard to do. He doesn't keep anything incriminating there, at least as far as I saw. I guess he never figured that anyone would learn anything from his answering machine. But I did. I heard your call about moving to this hotel."

Her hands were clenched tightly in her lap. "Oh, Jenny! If he ever found out you were in his place and listened to his machine, he'd be awfully angry."

I knew then that beneath her stubbornness she, too, was afraid. She, too, had a sense that there might be something else moving beneath the surface of things.

"Do you think Colin might find out you've come here? I mean, did you tell anyone?"

"No. I was very vague with my landlady. I told her I was going to stay with friends for a few days."

And out in the street I had tried to make sure that no one followed me. I walked several yards in the direction away from Victoria Station. When I saw a cab approaching I looked about quickly to see that there was no male pedestrian nearby and no one seated in a car parked at the curb. Then I hailed the cab and asked to be taken to Heathrow. I felt that even if someone had been spying on me, he would think it highly unlikely that I, a girl staying in about the cheapest accommodations London had to offer, would take a hideously expensive cab to Heathrow rather than the airport bus.

At Heathrow, though, I'd still tried to be careful. I observed who joined the ticket line after I did, and saw with relief that an elderly couple stood directly behind me, and, behind them, a woman with two small boys. Once I had my ticket I waited outside the gate. I was the last one to go through the boarding lounge onto the Paris-bound plane.

Yes, I felt that for an amateur I had been fairly adroit at eluding possible pursuit.

I leaned forward. "Betsy, listen to me! Let's go home. Let's go to the airport right now. I'm sure some airline will be running an afternoon or early-evening plane to New York. If not, we'll stay overnight at the airport hotel and leave the next day."

True, I was thinking, I had left a suitcase at Mrs. Ryan's, but I was sure she would ship it to me in New York.

"No!" All the stubbornness had come back into Betsy's face. "I think Colin's a crook and a chiseler and maybe an all-round heel, but it's not Colin I'm marrying."

"Betsy, please! You don't love that man. You'll have lots of time to marry, and lots and lots of chances."

109

"How do you know? What makes you such an authority? Things didn't turn out so good for you and Don Westin, did they?"

Don Westin was the man I'd been engaged to in Carrsville. Betsy wasn't often snide. I knew it was a measure of her own unsureness that she had brought up that old romantic misadventure of mine. And so I continued to bore in, asking her what proof she had that Antonio Braselmo was even married, let alone planning to divorce his wife and marry her.

Fists clenched, she hurled her answers at me. She knew he had a wife because she'd seen pictures of her and read letters she'd written to Tony. And how did she know he really was married to the woman who posed for the pictures and wrote the letters? Because she trusted him, that was how.

And finally she said what I suppose was the inevitable thing. "You're jealous, that's all. You know you'll never get a man like him, and so you're jealous."

My head had begun to throb. A leaden tiredness in my veins reminded me that I hadn't slept well the night before. I said, "Shall we call a truce for a while, Betsy? I've got to take a nap."

I could tell she regretted what she had said about jealousy. "All right. You do look beat."

"We'll go out to dinner in a couple of hours."

"Sure."

"You'll still be here when I wake up?"

Her face crumpled. "Oh, Jenny! Of course I'll be here."

TWELVE

At seven my sister and I walked to the Deux Magots on the Boulevard St. Germain. It was a café I had heard about, read about, and seen in a TV travelogue. Writers went there, and artists, and students from the nearby Sorbonne. The rain had stopped by then, and so we sat in the outdoor part of the café, not the part facing the boulevard but rather the seven-centuries-old church across an intersecting street. We sat in the corner well away from the few people on that side of the café.

We ordered onion soup, and toasted ham-and-cheese sandwiches, and glasses of red wine. And we continued to battle, repeating things we had said back at the hotel. All the time I felt a terrible sadness underneath. We were sisters. Each of us was the only family the other had left. It should have been so marvelous, our first evening at a Paris sidewalk café. And here we were, arguing bitterly about two slick, worldly men who, I felt, should never have had any place in the lives of the Carr Sisters from Carrsville, Missouri.

At last Betsy said, "Can't you understand? I see now that I can't have the sort of life I always wanted. But I'm not going to settle for just an ordinary life. I'm not, I'm not!"

With a rush of guilt, I did understand. Thanks largely to me, she'd grown up since preschool days with a gaudy dream. Elizabeth Carr curtseying to Her Majesty after a command performance at Covent Garden. Elizabeth Carr being led out by Baryshnikov for a sixth curtain call at Lincoln Center. Elizabeth Carr, watched by millions as she whirls across a stage before TV cameras.

That dream was smashed, and so she had turned to an even gaudier one that, over the past few years, had been the theme of so many novels, the dream about the woman who, thanks to her sexual allure, "has it all." Her personally designed perfume at one thousand dollars an ounce. Entree to the sort of store where, by appointment, she would be permitted to select hundred-dollar neckties for her husband or a five-thousand-dollar cashmere bathrobe. A Greek island that offered her friends a deep harbor for their yachts and, in the marble palace up on the hill, a jacuzzi with each of the twenty guest bedrooms.

"And don't you try to wreck things for me, Jenny! I swear that if you do I'll never speak to you again."

Did she mean it? I was sure she meant it at the moment. And she might go on meaning it for a long time. And she was all I had.

"Go home, Jenny. Go back to New York. Don't interfere. I'll write to you as soon as there is any news. I swear it."

There was no way to stop her. All I could do was to risk alienating her for years, or perhaps a lifetime.

Better to hope that the gaudy dream had a real foundation, after all, and that someday my sister would indeed be a familiar figure on Beverly Hills' Rodeo Drive, and Palm Beach's Worth Avenue, and Paris's Rue St. Honore.

"All right. I'll go home."

We walked back to the hotel and went up in the tiny elevator. In her room on the fifth floor we put our arms around each other and wept. "You really will write to me, Betsy?"

"Of course I will. And Jenny, don't be afraid that Colin will ever find out from me that you were here. I'd never do anything to—to cause you trouble."

"I know you wouldn't. Let's say good-bye now. I'll probably leave for the airport quite early."

The truth was that I felt I might start arguing with her if we talked in the morning, and I knew now that that would be futile.

We kissed, and I walked down the stairs to my fourth-floor room.

THIRTEEN

It was late afternoon of the next day by the time I walked up Ebury Street from Victoria Station. Cross-Channel flights had been crowded that day. I'd had to wait at the Paris airport several hours for an available seat.

As I moved along through the misty sunlight, I felt lonelier than ever before in my life. Lonely and helpless. I had a sharp longing to swallow my pride and call Mike Baker. But more than my pride was involved. There was the question of his own feelings. Obviously, he had resented the slur I had thrown at him. But perhaps after he thought it over he had been glad of it, because it had given him reason to withdraw from a troublesome situation. If that were the case, trying to reinvolve him in my plight would be not only unfair, but might turn out to be humiliatingly futile as well.

Carrying my tote bag, I went through the unlocked front door. Mike Baker was descending the stairs from the second floor.

He stopped short for an instant, and so did I, and then we hurried toward each other. At the foot of the stairs I went into his arms and he kissed me, a long kiss.

I went with him back up the stairs and unlocked my door. In the tiny sitting room he said, "This is the second time I've been here today. Your landlady has been out someplace. I hadn't a clue as to where you were. I thought perhaps you'd gone back to New York."

"No. Yesterday I went to Paris."

He said, after a moment, "Something to do with your sister?"

I nodded.

"You found her?"

"Yes."

"How did you—No, don't tell me now. We'll go to my flat, and I'll cook dinner for us, and then you can tell me the whole thing. Would you like that?"

Would I! I smiled at him, and then went down the hall to the bathroom. In the mirror above the washbasin I saw that I didn't look too great. No lipstick, hair in need of combing, freckles fully visible. But with a shaky smile I reflected that Mike hadn't seemed to mind. I used comb, liquid makeup, and lipstick. Then I rejoined Mike, and we left the rooming house. The Land-Rover was parked a little way up the street. Deep in my thoughts, I hadn't noticed it when I came in.

As we drove through the handsome London streets, where sunset lay warm on leafy squares and on white-pillared Georgian houses, we said nothing about my sister. But Mike did say, "For twenty-four hours I went on being sore at you. For another twenty-four I worried that you wouldn't forgive me for walking out. Then this morning

I woke up determined to straighten it out with you if I possibly could."

His third-floor walk-up was in a part of London that, he told me, was called St. John's Wood. It was just one big room with a cooking alcove. But the furniture was a pleasant mixture of traditional and modern—canvas director's chairs drawn up to a round golden oak dining table, a glass coffee table in front of a handsome Victorian sofa upholstered in red velvet, and a wide daybed covered with a paisley spread. Tall windows gave a view of trees across the road, bordering a canal where mallard ducks swam in the fading light. And between the windows, and running around three sides of the room, were photographs and color prints of steam locomotives, some sleek and powerful-looking, some absurd affairs with vertical boilers and pairs of enormous sidewheels.

I said, "You mentioned you liked steam engines, but I had no idea you liked them so much."

He smiled. "No one is mildly interested in steam. Either you think it is just an outdated form of transportation or you're crazy about it. The one you're looking at is Puffing Billy, one of the earliest British-made engines. It's in the Kensington Museum. Maybe we'll have a chance to look at it. The photograph to the right of Billy is Big Boy, an American engine. And next to that is a locomotive that drew the Orient Express back when the likes of Mata Hari rode it."

Although I set the table, Mike did the cooking. It was good, too. Baked potatoes with sour cream, medium-rare pepper steak, and a lettuce-and-tomato salad. With it we drank Italian red wine. We decided against the vanilla ice cream in the refrigerator.

117

When he had poured coffee, he said, "I think we'd better talk now."

"I guess we'd better." I spoke reluctantly. It had been pleasant just to enjoy this hour or so in this pleasant room with Mike, without thinking about how I happened to be here.

"First tell me how it was you went to Paris."

When I began to describe how I had climbed that outside staircase to Colin Bracely's flat Mike grew very still, but he said nothing. Nor did he interrupt while I told him of my stormy few hours with my young sister.

"There's nothing I can do," I said finally, "except hope that things will turn out the way she expects them to. I mean, all I can hope is that he really intends to marry her and treat her decently."

I paused, but still he said nothing. I asked, "Hadn't we better take care of the dishes?"

We did start to do the dishes. At least we carried them over to the sink in the little alcove. But then somehow we had turned to each other and were in each other's arms, mouths locked, and his fingers fumbling with the buttons of my blouse. Only moments later we were across the room on that wide daybed, and I was experiencing a pleasure that seemed so exquisite, and yet so natural, that my consciousness had no place for anything else.

When at last we lay quiet, my head on his bare shoulder, he said, "Hey! You're not spoken for, are you? Married? Engaged?"

"No. Are you?"

"Divorced. It was soon after I graduated from Cambridge. Neither of us had wanted to get married, but we thought we'd better. Then she learned she wasn't pregnant after all, and so we got divorced."

In spite of my worries, I felt so happy I wanted to cry. Mike hadn't asked me to marry him, but he would, eventually. Otherwise he wouldn't have mentioned the subject.

Head turned on the pillow, he was drawing a forefinger along to the bridge of my nose. I said, "I guess my freckles are showing."

"Yes. I like them."

"You do?"

"Very much so. Some chaps go for long hair, or dimples. I go for freckles." He paused, and then said abruptly, "I wish we didn't have to talk about your sister anymore tonight, but I'm going away tomorrow, and so we'd better."

I cried, "Away?"

"Just for three days. There's a film festival in Marrakech—Asiatic and Middle Eastern films—and my paper is sending me down there to cover it. And so we'd better talk about your sister now."

Again he paused, while my nerves tightened with apprehension. Then he said, "I told you my impression was that Antonio Braselmo was a bad boy. I didn't know just how bad. I've looked him up in my paper's morgue, and other papers', and I've been in touch with a man I know at Interpol. Braselmo is only one of the names he uses. He's been suspected of counterfeiting, gunrunning, and drug running, with now and then a flier in international prostitution. Suspected, hell! It's one of those cases where law-enforcement people are absolutely certain about his activities but, one way or another, have never managed to get an indictment.

"And so," he said, "we've got to get your sister away from him, somehow."

I cried, "But how? She wouldn't believe anything anyone says about him. He has her brainwashed."

"So I gathered. But we've got to find a way. I don't know what use he has for your sister. But I'm damned sure it isn't to make her Mrs. Antonio Braselmo. And even if it were, it scarcely would be what you'd call an enviable fate for an eighteen-year-old girl."

A shiver ran through me. He gathered me close. "Now I've already done something," he said. "We don't know where Braselmo is, but we do know where your cousin Colin is. I've put a tail on him."

"You mean someone is watching him?"

"Yes, a private detective I know who is very good, and who owes me a favor. I wrote a feature story about him once, and it resulted in some lucrative assignments for him.

"Now listen, Jenny. I want you to stay in your room after dark while I'm gone. And even in the daytime, don't go wandering about in the lonelier reaches of the British Museum, for instance. Stay with the crowds."

"I will. But I wish you didn't have to go away."

"So do I."

Perturbed as I was by what he had told me about Braselmo, I still had room for another concern. "Will there be starlets at the film festival?"

"Of course. A film festival without starlets would be like a circus without acrobats."

"I just hope none of them have freckles."

He smiled and kissed me. "These will be starlets from Japan and India and Pakistan. They don't have freckles."

We did the dishes before we left his flat the next morning. When we reached the Ebury Street house Michael climbed with me to the ground-floor hallway. He had just kissed me good-bye when Mrs. Ryan opened her door. From the look on her face it was obvious that she thought Michael was the "friend" with whom I'd gone away three days before, but she smiled pleasantly enough and wished us a good morning.

FOURTEEN

They were strange, those next three days. I was all by myself in a foreign city. And yet because I was in love with Mike now, and fairly sure that he was in love with me, I did not feel lonely. Worried and apprehensive, yes, but not lonely.

I kept my promise to "stay with the crowds." I took a bus tour to Windsor Castle, and admired all that china George the Fourth bought, and on the return trip to London I looked through the bus window at the field where the barons had forced wayward King John to sign a promise to be less so. I took a sight-seeing boat down the Thames to Greenwich, past the pub where Mike and I had dined, past another pub from where, according to the public address system, Hanging Judge Jeffreys had watched chained prisoners on the opposite bank wait for death by drowning in the advancing tide, and past the Tower of London, which from the water looked so gala with white walls and wind-whipped bright banners that it was hard to realize that for centuries men and women had suffered torture and death here.

Betsy was never far from the surface of my thoughts, of course. Again and again I had an almost overwhelming urge to telephone that Left Bank hotel, just to ask whoever answered if Miss Nancy Allen of Detroit was still there. But she would be almost certain to hear of it. And then she might disappear again, this time to someplace where I might not be able to find her.

As for my anxiety about my own safety, I didn't realize how keen it was until the third night after Mike's departure. For dinner that evening I had gone to the pub near Mrs. Ryan's, the same pub where Colin and I had talked a few days earlier. When I left, around eight, the daylight was fading.

I had gone only a few yards when I heard rapid footsteps behind me. With a nervous leap of my heart I looked back. A man, a tall man with a hat-shadowed face, was striding toward me in obvious pursuit. For an instant I stood rooted, unable to scream or to turn and dart up the steps of the nearest house.

He raised his hand, waved something. "You left your book, miss."

I managed to say "Thank you" and hold out a shaking hand for the paperbacked catalogue, bought that afternoon at the Tate Gallery, which I had been reading while I had dinner. He tipped his hat and walked back to the pub.

When I reached my room my heart was still racing. And the next morning, still jittery, and hoping that Mike had returned and would soon telephone, I did not go out for breakfast, but instead used the hot plate to heat water for tea-bag tea. With it I ate a concoction, purchased from a bakery the day before, which the woman behind the counter had called a sticky bun.

Mike called about one o'clock. Would I meet him at a place near his office for a late lunch?

When I walked into the restaurant, a very English place with time-blackened oak walls and dazzlingly white starched tablecloths, I saw by the way Mike's sleepy-looking eyes lit up that, starlets or no starlets, he'd missed me. I also sensed that, below the surface, he was far more keyed-up than he had been when we said good-bye four mornings earlier.

While we ate flounder and cauliflower and green peas, I asked him about the film festival. Most of them were musicals, he said, and quite dreadful, although one documentary about a family who lived on a Calcutta sidewalk was sure to win some international prizes. Then he said abruptly, "I stopped over in Paris this morning. Your sister is still at that hotel."

I cried, alarmed, "You didn't—"

"Of course I didn't go to the hotel. I never left the Paris airport."

"Then how—"

"The Paris police. Police in any city will cooperate with journalists, at least to a certain extent. From Marrakech I phoned this flic I'd had contact with in the past, and asked him to find out on the quiet if an American girl registered as Nancy Allen was still at the Hotel du Rivage. It's easy for them. They just send a gendarme around with some vague story about a routine check on the guest list of hotels in that district. Anyway, when I phoned the Sûreté during a layover at the Paris airport this morning, I learned she was still there."

I thought of her in that obscure hotel, waiting for word from the man who would lift her into his world, a world where no one ever stayed anywhere except the Ritz or the Savoy or the Waldorf Towers.

"You didn't learn anything else?"

He shook his head. Then he broke a breadstick in half and laid it on his plate. Seeming to forget about it, he said, "Jenny, I'm going to have to go away again."

"No!" I thought of my unease these past few days, an unease that had sharpened to panic when a kindly stranger pursued me with a forgotten book. "Where are you going?"

"Switzerland. I'll fly to Zurich two days from now and then take the train to Interlaken."

"But why?"

"To interview Davey Wanderer."

"The rock star?"

"Yes. He's going to set up a place for homeless kids in Switzerland. Sort of an international Boys' Town."

"Take me with you!"

"Jenny, that's not practical."

"Why not? What's wrong with my riding in the same plane and the same train?"

"Why do you want to so much?"

I told him of my absurd panic the night before on Ebury Street. I saw conflict in Michael's eyes. "I can see why you don't want to be alone here. But there are also reasons why . . ."

His voice trailed off. I said, "There's something you're not telling me, isn't there?" Then, with an intuitive leap, "It's about Betsy, isn't it?"

The look in his eyes told me that the answer was yes. He picked up a breadstick half, laid it down again. "All

126

right. I don't *have* to interview Davey Wanderer. The assignment went originally to another staff member. But about an hour ago I persuaded him to let me take it over."

"But why? What's your real reason for going to—"

"Have you heard of a Belgian named Armand Perrault?"

I frowned. "Isn't he one of the world's richest men?"

"Yes. Shipping, mainly. He's very old now, of course. He'd already been retired for some time when I saw him about a dozen years ago."

"You interviewed him then?"

"No. I was still at Cambridge in those days. He'd invited me to come to Switzerland during my vacation to see him, or rather, his engines. I'd been corresponding with him about them."

"Engines?"

"Steam locomotives. In a valley near Interlaken he has the largest private collection in the world."

"And he's the one you really want to see in Switzerland?"

He nodded.

"Then why bother with Davey Wanderer?"

"Because somebody called the paper while I was in Marrakech, somebody who wanted to know where I was. He didn't leave his name."

"You think it could have been Colin?"

"Perhaps. Of course, it could have been just some old Cambridge friend, wanting to get back in touch. Just the same, if someone calls this time, I want him to hear that I've gone to see Davey Wanderer, not Armand Perrault.

"I'm sure he'll agree to see me," Michael went on. "Oh, not as a journalist. Perrault never gives interviews or even sees many visitors. But we still correspond about steam

127

from time to time. He'll see me because of that."

I sat in bewildered silence for a moment. What could a billionaire steam-train buff have to do with my reckless little sister? I asked, "Why do you want to see this man?"

"Because Perrault has a private secretary, a man who's been with him for the past twenty-five years. His name is Rogers, Stanfield Rogers. He was in London two days ago, staying at the Connaught. Your cousin went to see him there and spent more than an hour in his room."

"Colin did? How do you know? You weren't even in London two days ago."

"Remember I told you that I had asked a man I know, a private investigator who owes me a favor, to keep an eye on your cousin? Well, that's how I know. I phoned my friend as soon as I landed at Heathrow this morning and he told me about the Connaught visit."

I thought of my no-good cousin entering that haughty hotel, rising in its lift to call upon a reclusive billionaire's private secretary, and discuss with him—what?

I said slowly, "And you think all this has something to do with Betsy?"

"I think it must."

"Why? It seems to me it could be about something else entirely." I paused. "Or do you have other reasons for thinking it's all tied in with Betsy?"

"You really think I need another reason?"

He'd spoken quickly enough, and with no flicker of expression on his poker face. But I felt sure he was lying to me, or at least evading me. He *did* have some additional reason to think that Colin's interview with the old man's secretary concerned my sister.

But I decided not to try to get past Mike's evasion, lest

it only increase his unwillingness to take me to Switzerland. And now, more than ever, I wanted to go with him.

"Please, Mike. Please take me with you. I'll be more uneasy than ever if I'm left alone in London."

After a long moment he said, "I can see why you would be, maybe with reason. Maybe I'd feel easier in my mind, too, if you were with me. All right, you can come."

FIFTEEN

Our compartment on the Zurich-to-Interlaken train was empty except for ourselves. Thus there was no one to complain that we had pulled the window down, allowing frigid air off the towering slopes to flow into this small, moving room.

In my own country, I had never been more than a hundred miles west of the Mississippi. Thus these Alps were the first really high mountains I had ever seen. I understood now why people once had believed mountains to be the homes of gods, or even gods themselves. Some cloud-wreathed, some with sunlight sparkling on their icy slopes, they reared against the early-afternoon sky, more beautiful than anything I had ever seen, and yet so awesome that I felt something like fear.

Now and then the valley through which the train ran widened out. Then I saw vineyards and still-leafy fruit orchards down along the riverbank. I also saw cattle of a breed strange to me, with hides the light brown color of milk chocolate. The musical sound of the bells hung around their necks was sometimes distinguishable through the clatter of the train's wheels. Occasionally there were hamlets, with churches whose onion-shaped domes were a reminder that Eastern Europe and its Greek Orthodox Catholicism were not far away.

Around one-thirty the train drew into Interlaken, a storybook-pretty resort town with the mighty Jungfrau towering in the distance. At the car-rental office at the station, where Mike arranged to pick up a VW later in the afternoon, we learned that Davey Wanderer's hotel was only a couple of hundred yards away. We walked up a sloping street past small ski-supply shops, and houses with steeply pitched roofs to shed the winter snows, and gardens where, although it was now early October, dahlias and gladiolas and even second-bloom roses flourished, an odd contrast to the eternal ice and snow visible on the Jungfrau's upper slope. At this in-between season, apparently, not many people came to Interlaken. The street was uncrowded and so was the lobby of Davey Wanderer's hotel.

He met us at the door of his fifth-floor room. With its long windows opening onto a balcony, the room looked impressive. Davey did not. Betsy and I had attended a Manhattan concert of his soon after we moved into that Queens apartment. Guitar slung from a cord around his neck, and backed by four other musicians, he had seemed to dominate the stage and the audience completely, whether the song was a gentle ballad or a snarl of rebellion. Now, in jeans and a white cotton shirt instead of silver leather, and with his blond hair brushed flat rather than standing up in spikes, he seemed slighter, younger, and even a bit shy.

His shyness dropped away, though, when he began to talk of the children's home. He spread blueprints on the floor and reeled off numbers—building costs, projected yearly upkeep, and children to be accommodated.

Later Mike began to ask him about his childhood when, as plain David Jones, he had grown up in a Welsh coal-mining town. I knew that most of Mike's thoughts, like mine, must be centered on the coming visit to Armand Perrault. But Mike was good at his job. From the look on his face one would have thought that he was giving his entire attention to Davey's account of how, as a young boy, he had watched his father and older brothers scrub and scrub, and yet never dislodge the coal dust entirely from the creases in their necks.

Around two-thirty we said good-bye, walked back to the station, and picked up the VW. Mike drove east for about two miles and then turned off onto a much narrower road that led upward, with many switchbacks, through pine-clad hills. We had been on the sideroad about ten minutes when he guided the car off between a break in the trees and then turned off the engine.

"What—" I said. Then I understood.

We waited in silence for three minutes, four, five. No car appeared. Mike visibly relaxed. Perhaps it was thanks to the Davey Wanderer ruse. Anyway, whether or not we had been under surveillance in London, no one was watching us here. Mike started the engine and drove back to the road.

Soon it became apparent that there had been a recent

snowfall at these heights. It had melted, though, except for an occasional bluish-white patch under a pine. Then the trees began to thin, and I realized that we must be nearing the timberline.

Mike turned off onto a still narrower road, one which ran along a rocky spur almost bare of vegetation. Beyond the valleys on either side of us rose wave upon wave of snow-clad Alps. And perhaps half a mile ahead, its many windows sparkling in the sunlight, stood a white stone structure so large that it might have been a hotel, except that no one would build a hotel in this isolated spot at the end of a road not much wider than the little car we drove.

I asked, "Armand Perrault's house?"

Mike nodded.

A little daunted by those scores of windows, and those red-tile roofs on several levels, I asked, "Are you sure we're not too early?"

"We'll be right on the nose. When I phoned him yesterday I asked if he could see us at three, so that we'd have time to take the train back to Zurich and catch an evening flight for London."

Moments later, he stopped the VW at the foot of stone steps that fanned out from massive double doors of intricately carved wood. Almost instantly one of the doors opened and a red-haired young man in a swallow-tailed green coat, fawn-colored knee breeches, and striped stockings hurried down to open the car door. I realized he must be a footman, the first one I had ever encountered except in a movie or on a TV screen.

At the top of the stairs, an older man in a butler's black suit and striped black-and-white waistcoat bowed us inside. We followed him across a semicircular foyer floor of brown, pink-veined marble, past the foot of a double stairway, and then along a wide hall. On either side, partially opened doors gave me a glimpse of oriental carpets, gleaming mahogany, crystal chandeliers. Finally we stepped out onto a terrace, rounded like the stern of some enormous ship, and bathed in midafternoon sunlight. On two sides of it, like gigantic waves about to overwhelm us, rose jagged, snow-capped Alps.

One blue-veined hand pressing down on the head of a cane, the other on the arm of his white wrought-iron chair, a bald man who looked to be well past eighty got to his feet. You could tell he had been quite tall before the years rounded his shoulders. You could also tell he had been handsome, with gray eyes under prominent brow ridges, a prowlike nose, and well-cut mouth and square chin.

He said, "How good to see you, Mr. Baker!" I would never have placed his accent. Perhaps it was Belgian. More likely it was the accent of a European who had learned many languages. As they shook hands, I could tell that the old man was genuinely glad to see Mike.

"Jenny," Mike said, turning to me, "this is Monsieur Perrault. Miss Carr, monsieur."

We sat down, the Belgian in his chair and Mike and I on a wrought-iron settee with a cretonne-covered cushion. The butler took our respective requests for drinks—Campari for Mike and me, iced tea for Mr. Perrault—and a few minutes later a brunette maid of about twenty brought them to us.

For a while the old man courteously included me in the conversation, asking if this was my first trip to Switzerland, where I lived in the States, and so on. But it was obvious that he was eager to get past the small talk to the subject of real interest to him. Finally he said to Mike, "Did you hear that some more Chapelon four-eight-twos have been found?"

"Yes. In an abandoned freight yard in Yugoslavia, wasn't it?"

Then they were off, talking of front-driving axles and lateral reaction and piston valve settings and equally arcane topics. Scarcely listening, I leaned back, looked at clouds drifting across the most deeply blue sky I had ever seen, and breathed air that, at this height, seemed at least as intoxicating as the mild drink I sipped.

At last I heard Monsieur Perrault say, "Then shall we go down to visit my treasures?"

Mike said, "I'd like that very much."

"Good, we'll go down in the funicular car. That will be much quicker than driving down in a Jeep. Would you care to accompany us, Miss Carr?"

I was sure he didn't want someone along whose ignorant or frivolous questions he, out of courtesy, would have to answer. Nor did I want to go. Steam locomotives ranked somewhere below frog-jumping contests on my scale of interests.

"If you don't mind, I would rather wait here in this marvelous sunshine."

"Just as you like, mademoiselle. If you desire anything, push the button beside the doorway."

When the two men had disappeared inside the house, I sat for several minutes, face upturned to the sun's warmth. Then I walked over to the waist-high stone wall that encircled the terrace. A small telescope had been mounted upon it. From there I could see down into the valley running along one side of the rocky spur. And although the valley was deep in shadow, once I looked through the telescope I could make them out down there in a space cleared of trees, a score or more steel monsters that once had roared across flatlands and over bridges and through mountain tunnels, now immobilized forever in this remote spot. It seemed to me sad, like an elephant graveyard. Also, as I peered down at smokestacks and huge sidewheels and headlights, I began to feel a dim understanding of what attracted people so powerfully to steam locomotives. I swung the telescope a little to the left and saw a funicular car sliding down toward a metal tower that rose above a clump of evergreens.

A clinking sound behind me on the terrace. I turned to see the pretty brunette maid. Tray in hand, she was gathering up from the white wrought-iron table the glasses we had used.

I smiled at her and she smiled back. She said, in accented English, "You look at the engines, miss?"

I nodded, still smiling.

"Is strange, no, to see engines in such a place?" I caught the impression that young visitors to this house were rare, and so she was eager to prolong the conversation with someone near her own age.

"Very strange."

"Can you guess how Monsieur Perrault brought them there?"

Startled, I said, "Why, I hadn't even thought to wonder about it."

"Here, I show you." She set down the tray and crossed the terrace to stand beside me. Even though I no longer looked through the telescope, I could see that the funicular car had reached its landing tower. After a moment

I saw that Mike and the old man stood beside an engine whose brass fittings gleamed dully in the valley's shadowy depths.

"First," the girl said, "Monsieur Perrault builded side tracks from the—How do you say it?"

"Main railroad line?"

"Yes. From there he builded tracks to that place down there. Then he bring engines he buy all over Europe. Then he tear up the side rails. Why I don't know. Maybe he afraid someone will come at night and drive his engines away." Whether or not she was poking gentle fun at her employer I couldn't tell.

"Anyway," she went on, "this was long time ago, long before I come here, but you can still see break in trees where track were."

You could. The trees that filled the narrow valley had not grown enough to obscure completely the path that had been cleared to accommodate the rails. From the terrace it looked as if a giant finger had drawn a furrow through the treetops.

I thought of how much money he must have spent to have those rails laid, only to order them torn up. I said, "Monsieur Perrault must be fond indeed of locomotives."

"Oh, yes! And he is also very, very rich." She paused and then said, "I could show you some of the house before the gentlemen return. Monsieur Perrault would not mind."

"Thank you." As we walked back across the terrace I asked, "What is your name?"

"Angelique."

She showed me a gun room, filled with what appeared to me to be enough rifles to outfit a regiment, all in glass cases. We looked into a dining room that could have ac-

commodated at least thirty people at a rectangular mahogany table, and a drawing room filled with delicate
French armchairs and settees and graceful-legged mar-
quetry tables. Then Angelique said, "This is Monsieur
Perrault's favorite room."

It was a library, lined from floor to ceiling with books
on three sides and part of a fourth. The rest of the fourth
wall was taken up by a fireplace in its center, a six-feet-
wide one with a black marble mantel. The rug, an Oriental
in muted reds and blues and earth tones, was of a size I
heretofore had seen only in photographs of some OPEC
ruler's palace. The furniture, though, mostly brown leather
sofas and settees, was almost shabby, at least in compar-
ison to everything else I had seen.

The only picture in the room hung above the mantel.
It was the portrait of a blond, blue-eyed little girl in a
white dress, sitting with one white-socked leg tucked under
her in a high-backed chair upholstered in dark blue velvet.
As I looked at it I felt an odd, premonitory tightening of
my nerves.

Angelique said, "That was Monsieur's granddaughter.
Her name was Nicole."

"Was? You mean she died?"

Angelique spread expressive hands. "Who can say? That
is the saddest part of it. No one knows what happen to
her, because she was kidnapped."

I said, after an interval, "When did this happen?"

"Oh, a long time ago, long before I come here. Fifteen
years ago, I think. I was young myself then, too young to
remember. But later I hear how he pay millions in ransom,
but never get his little granddaughter back. And think,
mademoiselle, she was only family he have. His wife died

many years ago. His son, the father of little Nicole, he and his wife are lost in plane crash. Is very sad."

She paused, and then said, "Here is another picture of Nicole."

I walked with her over to a leather-topped table that bore several miniatures. Angelique handed me an oval one, painted on ivory and framed in what I am sure was real gold. Heart beating fast, I looked down at it. A portrait of the child's head and shoulders, it apparently had been painted at about the same time as the large picture.

Unless the painter had erred, Nicole Perrault had had a fleck of green in her right eye.

I replaced the miniature on the table. Nerves tight, I walked close to the portrait above the mantel. In this larger picture, too, the artist had painted that wedge-shaped bit of green.

I turned around. "How old was the little girl when she was kidnapped?"

"Only four, mademoiselle. Think of it!"

Four years old fifteen years ago. If she was still alive, Nicole would be only a little older than my sister.

I could hear the blood drumming in my ears now. Had my cousin and Antonio Braselmo convinced this enormously rich old man that Nicole Perrault *was* alive? I was sure of it. That was why Armand Perrault had sent his long-trusted private secretary to London to confer with my cousin.

I thought of my sister in that Paris hotel, confidently waiting for Antonio Braselmo to get his divorce and marry her. And all the time those two men, Braselmo and Colin, had quite different plans for her. . . .

Suddenly I felt weak, even a little nauseated. I said, "I think I'll go back onto the terrace."

I must have grown pale, because Angelique asked, "You are *malade*, mademoiselle?"

"No. I just feel the need of air."

She accompanied me out onto the terrace, picked up her trays, and then, after I had assured her I wanted nothing, went back into the house. I stood at the terrace balustrade. The aerial tramcar was returning now, a cool silvery shape at first, and then, as it emerged from the valley's shadow, a flashing mirror for the afternoon sun.

What should I do? Confront the old man as soon as he returned, demand to know the nature of his communications with my cousin? That was what I wanted desperately to do. But caution told me that I had best confer with Michael first. Otherwise, in my ignorance, I might only increase whatever peril my sister was in.

By the time the two men walked out on the terrace, I was in sufficient control of myself to say yes, I had been enjoying the sunshine and the view. But ten minutes later, after we had said good-bye to Monsieur Perrault and driven perhaps a mile along that rocky spur, I said, "Mike, please stop."

He turned a startled face toward me, then stopped the car. "What is it?"

"I think perhaps we should go back and talk to Armand Perrault."

"Go back, when we've a train to catch at Interlaken?"

"We must talk to him about his granddaughter." The look that leaped into his eyes made me add, "You knew about his granddaughter, didn't you?"

141

"That she was kidnapped? Yes. It happened about three years before I met him. I was in my first year at Cambridge then. It was big news all over Europe and in England." He paused. "I gather you didn't know about it until today."

"No, I didn't know." I had been only eleven at that time, and besides, a small Missouri town was a long way from Switzerland.

"Then how is it—"

"That maid who served our drinks." I told him about going back to the library and seeing the large portrait and the miniature of Nicole.

I said, gaze steady on his face, "And you also knew that Nicole Perrault was blond and blue-eyed, with a greenish fleck in her right eye."

"Yes. After the kidnappers had collected the ransom but failed to return her, Armand Perrault saw to it that the child's description was circulated as widely as possible."

"And it was because you knew that my sister was about the same age as the Perrault girl would be, and blond like her, and with eyes like hers—I mean, that was why you were so sure that Betsy was the reason for that meeting between Perrault's secretary and Colin."

Mike nodded. I cried, "Then why didn't you tell me all this?"

"Because I didn't want to worry you any more than I had to. It was hard enough on you when you thought your sister was going to marry a man like Braselmo. I didn't want to speak until I had to about what I really suspected."

"That he and my cousin were going to try to palm Betsy off on that old man as his granddaughter?"

Mike nodded.

I said, "But it won't work! Betsy would have to cooperate. And she never would. Oh, I'm not saying she's any paragon. She's lied to herself, convinced herself that she's in love with this man, when all she really wants is what she thinks he will give her. But she wouldn't deceive a grieving old man, not for anything."

And then I stopped short. Perhaps it was something in his face that caused me to realize that there could be ways to make her do things. She could be drugged, or threatened . . .

I said, "The way to stop them is to go back there right now and tell that old man the truth." I paused. "Or have you already told him?"

"No."

I cried, "Why not?"

"Don't you see? He must want desperately to believe that his granddaughter is still alive. If I told him that Braselmo and Braccly were planning to palm off on him some other young girl, he would immediately challenge them. And they, afraid he would go to the police, might decide to get rid of the evidence."

The evidence. My sister.

I said, hands clenched in my lap, "Why did you want to come here today?"

"I had to make sure that my hunch about your sister and that kidnapped child was correct. And I did make sure."

"How?"

"Nearly all the time we discussed locomotives. But finally I made a reference to Nicole Perrault. While we were inspecting a French locomotive, I said, 'This one was on the Paris-to-Venice run until the summer your granddaughter was kidnapped, wasn't it?' I was looking straight at him as I spoke, and I saw, not the pain one might have expected, but a look of pure joy.

"I apologized for reminding him of a past tragedy, and he said, smiling, 'You are forgiven, *mon ami.*' I was sure then that he is expecting to have Nicole back with him soon."

For perhaps a minute there was no sound except the faint keening of wind across the rocky spur. Then I asked, "What are we going to do?"

"Go back to London."

"And then?"

"I'll need to check on things. Check with my friend who's keeping an eye on your cousin. Check with that Paris policeman who sent someone around to your sister's hotel. But Jenny, will you let me handle it, without asking me a lot of questions? Will you trust me?"

Trust him. In this strange world in which Betsy had landed herself—and me—whom else did I have to trust?

"All right," I said.

SIXTEEN

We landed at Heathrow a little before ten that night. It was almost midnight when we climbed the stairs to Michael's flat in St. John's Wood. True to my promise, I asked no more questions. But long after our lovemaking, long after the slow rhythm of his breath as he lay beside me told me that he was asleep, I kept thinking, there's something else, something even worse, something he hasn't told me yet.

In the morning, over toast and scrambled eggs, he said, "Will you just wait, Jenny?"

"Wait until what?"

"Until I have the pieces fitted together, so to speak. Will you just wait until I phone you?"

Again, what else could I do? "I'll wait," I said.

He drove me to Ebury Street. I climbed the front steps alone and walked into the cabbage-smelling entrance hall. I did not see Mrs. Ryan, although I could hear her TV through her closed apartment door.

Mike telephoned late that afternoon, but his call was brief and noncommital. He would call again, he said, when he had something "definite" to tell me.

I spent a wretched night, asking myself questions I could not answer. How much had Armand Perrault agreed to pay Braselmo and my cousin for restoring his granddaughter to him? Millions, undoubtedly.

And could I be so sure, after all, that those two would have to drug my sister, or otherwise coerce her, in order to get her to go along with their highly profitable hoax? Betsy had amply demonstrated that she was capable of self-deception. She had convinced herself, aided considerably by my own delusions on the subject, that she had the makings of a world-class ballerina.

Later she had persuaded herself that she loved Antonio Braselmo and that he loved her, with only his still-pending divorce standing between them. Would it be so hard for her to accept now the idea of becoming, not Braselmo's wife, but the beloved heir of one of the world's richest men? After all, it might be that she could convince herself that she was doing the old man a favor.

I wondered, too, about what had happened to her, that lost little girl. Almost certainly, she was dead. But what story had those two given the old man about where his "granddaughter" had spent the last fifteen years? Perhaps they had told him that the child had been found, apparently abandoned by the kidnappers, at some remote spot in the United States, and had been raised by an American couple, now dead. No matter what fantastic story they had told him, it had been obvious from his behavior with Michael that he had accepted it, probably because he wanted so much for it to be true.

Michael. I recalled his unrevealing face as he said good-bye to me that morning at the foot of the rooming-house steps. And again I had a sense that he was withholding something from me, something even more dreadful than he had told me so far.

I went to sleep, finally, only to awake to another long day of waiting. The light had begun to fade by the time Mike called. He would pick me up in fifteen minutes.

When I opened the door to him I felt I could see at least faint signs of tension in that usually unreadable face. But on the way through evening traffic to St. John's Wood, I managed to fight down my need to question him.

In his flat he poured two Campari and sodas. Then, as we sat on that Victorian sofa, our drinks resting on the glass coffee table, he said abruptly, "Your sister is no longer in Paris."

My heart jumped. "Where—"

"Someplace in Scotland, more than likely."

I said nothing, but just looked at him, hands clenched in my lap.

"I phoned my cop friend in Paris, and he had someone check the hotel. It seems that your sister left there yesterday morning. The elderly desk clerk followed her out to the sidewalk to say good-bye, and heard her ask the taxi driver to take her to L'Erable. That's a town with a private airfield, about fifteen miles from Paris."

I could imagine that badly smitten hotel clerk, wanting to stay in Betsy's company until the last possible moment.

"I called the L'Erable airfield. They told me that a commercial pilot named Douvier had filed a flight plan for Clairgowrie, Scotland. Then he'd taken off with a young woman passenger."

147

"This Clairgowrie," I managed to ask. "Where is it in Scotland?"

"North of Inverness."

"And after they landed at Clairgowrie, where—"

"All I could find out when I phoned the man at the Clairgowrie field was that the pilot flew back alone to France. The airfield attendant I spoke to hadn't been on duty at the time, but the man who had been on duty then told him that the passenger, a blond girl, had been picked up by a man and driven away."

"*What* man?" When Michael shook his head, I asked, "Colin?"

"Probably. I checked with my friend who's been keeping an eye on your cousin. Colin Bracely took the train to Edinburgh yesterday. I haven't been able to confirm that he rented a car in Edinburgh. The rental agency at the railroad station had no record of a Bracely, but he could have rented under another name, and then picked up your sister."

"And Braselmo?"

"I can't know for sure, but I think he must be in Scotland, too, or will be shortly."

"*Where* in Scotland?"

"Jenny, I don't know. I just know that the Highlands are filled with remote glens, some of them reachable only on foot or over roads that are just two tracks. I think they've taken your sister to some sort of dwelling, probably a stone croft, in one of those glens."

"But why?"

After a moment he said, "To wait." He reached out and took both my hands in his. I thought, my every nerve

148

shrinking: *It's coming now, that thing he's been holding back.*

He said, "When Armand Perrault circulated the description of his kidnapped granddaughter, he listed another identification mark besides that green fleck in one eye. The child also had a clubfoot."

I don't know what I had expected him to tell me, but not that. Disconcerted, not grasping the significance of what he had said, I thought of the portrait of that little girl, sitting in the high-backed chair with one foot tucked beneath her.

"That girl—the maid, I mean—she said nothing about Nicole Perrault being lame."

"Maybe it didn't occur to her to mention it. More likely, she'd forgotten about it, or had never known about it. She must have been only a very young child at the time of the kidnapping."

"But why hadn't the child's foot been taken care of soon after her birth? Surely an operation—"

"Like so many babies with birth defects, Nicole had been premature and quite frail. Doctors had advised that she not be operated on until her fifth year. She had just turned four when she disappeared."

So that was why. Then I cried, "But Mike! Listen! This means they can't be planning to palm Betsy off as his granddaughter. Betsy doesn't have a clubfoot, or ever did have—"

Then it hit me, like a fist slamming into the pit of my stomach. Michael was aware that now I understood. I could tell by the way his hands tightened around mine.

I whispered, "You think they're waiting up there for a—a surgeon, don't you?"

"I think so. I think Braselmo has been looking for one and finally found him. That's why your cousin had Betsy brought from that Paris hotel."

That hotel. They'd kept her there to give Braselmo time, not to finalize a divorce from a vindictive wife, but to find a man of medicine depraved enough, or desperate enough . . .

Then I cried, "But it can't be. If they did that to Betsy, if they—they deformed her, she would never go along with them, no matter what they threatened." And no matter how alluring the prospect of becoming a billionaire's heir. To Betsy her dancing feet, even though she knew now they could never carry her to Covent Garden, would still be worth more than all the money in the world.

"Don't you see? If they did that to her, she would reveal the whole thing the moment they left her with Armand Perrault. And so it must be that you're all wrong about what they intend—"

The look in his eyes stopped me. After a moment he said, "I can see by your face that you've understood. They don't intend to give her a chance to tell Perrault or anyone else the truth."

I managed to move my lips. "Then how? Some kind of—movie?"

He nodded. "That must be it. They must have managed to get the old man to agree to pay them as soon as they delivered absolute proof that they could bring his granddaughter back to him. A movie of a girl walking around, a girl of the right age and coloring, with a green fleck in

150

her eye, and, clinching it all, a deformed foot—that ought to be absolute proof."

And after that? After Braselmo and Colin Bracely had collected the millions they would simply disappear, first having made sure that Betsy Carr would never be able to talk to Armand Perrault, or the police, or anyone else.

I said, "You've gone to the police?"

"No."

"Why not?" My voice rose high and thin. I tried to jerk my hands free of his. "Why not?"

"It would be a waste of time, and wasting time is something we mustn't do."

"A waste of—"

"Yes! We have no more evidence now than before that a crime was committed, or is about to be. Was it a crime for a girl to be flown as an obviously willing passenger from a French airfield to a Scottish one? Was it a crime for Colin Bracely, under whatever name, to meet that same girl and drive off with her?"

When I didn't answer he said, "Of course it isn't. And it won't be a crime for Antonio Braselmo to fly from Lord knows where to Scotland, if he hasn't already. It won't be a crime for that surgeon to go up there. The crime won't occur until after he arrives."

I said, trying to control my panic, "You don't think the doctor is up there already?"

"No. I may be wrong about this, but I think Braselmo has had a hell of a time finding a man with sufficient skill and depravity for a job like this. Once Braselmo did find this man—well, I imagine he must have demanded more than a considerable amount of money. He must have dic-

151

tated conditions. He'd want a room prepared for his work. He might want the—patient to have been tranquilized, not just for several hours but for several days, so she'd give him no trouble. And he'd want to be able to get away as soon as his work was done. Making such arrangements would require a certain amount of time."

That sick feeling in the pit of my stomach was more intense now. I asked, "How long after that will they—will they—"

"Her foot would have to heal at least somewhat before they could make a convincing film. Not completely heal. Makeup could conceal any too-fresh scars. Besides, that old man will be so eager to believe what they show him. Still, a certain amount of time will have to elapse between the operation and the filmmaking. My guess is that if they have a place they regard as safe, they'll keep her there during the interval."

"What—what are you—what are we—I mean, shouldn't we tell Perrault what we suspect? A man with his influence might be able to—"

"The old man would never believe us, at least not in time. He must be so sure that those two can restore his granddaughter to him. Too, they must have threatened him, told him that if he talks to the police or anyone else the whole deal will be off.

"As I see it," he went on, "there's only one thing to do. I must try to find wherever it is that they have taken her. Perhaps once I know that, I can figure out some effective way of calling the police in."

"Take me with you!"

"Jenny, there's no time to be lost. I want to be in

Edinburgh by daylight. That means I'll have to start driving—"

"I can be ready as soon as you say!"

Those heavy-lidded eyes studied me. Then he said, "Lord knows I'll probably be able to use some help. And if the going gets too rough . . ."

He looked at his watch. "If I drive you back to Ebury Street, can you dress warmly, pack a few things in that shoulder tote of yours, and be ready to leave an hour and a half from now?"

I nodded.

SEVENTEEN

The shrill of a traffic policeman's whistle awoke me. With my eyes still closed I was aware of the car's motion, and of my cramped limbs as I sat curled in one corner of the front seat, and of mist cool on my face.

I opened my eyes. A broad avenue, bordered with trees still in leaf. Over its glistening pavement early traffic moved at a brisk pace. And up ahead, through the mist, loomed gray-stoned battlements and towers that I had seen again and again in photographs.

I sat up. Michael shot me a brief smile. I asked, "Edinburgh?"

"Yes. Did you sleep fairly well?"

I nodded, then took out my comb and pocket mirror and peered at my pale, still sleepy face. It had been a strange night. I had helped him pack the car's trunk—or boot, as Michael called it—with a double sleeping bag, flashlights, a Thermos, and a small primus stove. He had bought most of that equipment the previous summer, he told me, before he and a friend went on a rock-climbing trip near Ullswater. He did not mention the sex of the friend, nor did I ask. Once the camping gear was stowed, we drove to Ebury Street. Mrs. Ryan must have been watching an old movie on TV, because from behind her closed door came the sound of Humphrey Bogart's voice. I climbed the stairs, changed to wool pants and my heaviest sweater, and packed my tote bag.

By midnight we left London's northern suburbs with their semidetached villas and darkened shops behind us and were driving along M-I. "Try to sleep," Michael told me. And after a while I did manage to doze, although I never entirely lost consciousness of motion, and the engine's hum, and the huge lorries that rocked the car with the wind of their passing. Too, I sometimes felt a strange awareness, almost as if by some racial memory of my Anglo-Saxon ancestors, that the land over which we moved so easily and swiftly had been traversed slowly, laboriously, painfully, and sometimes bloodily by Britons and Roman legionnaires and invading Norsemen. In fact, I had a confused dream in which Michael and I in the Land-Rover joined King John and his plumed knights in an effort to cross a body of water that somehow I knew was the Wash. I also knew that at any moment a cart was to overturn, spilling gems and gold bars into the swift water, where they would be lost forever. But before that could happen the blast of a diesel lorry's horn brought me momentarily awake.

Now we had turned onto one of the handsomest streets I had ever seen. On the left rose tall buildings of gray stone. To the right, below the level of the street, stretched a garden bright with multicolored chrysanthemums. Now that I was awake, all my anxiety flooded back. Neverthe-less, I was aware of this city's gray and ancient beauty. And when Michael told me that a tall tower of intricately carved stone down there among the flower beds was a monument to Sir Walter Scott, I was able to feel, despite my worries, a stir of admiration for a people who built large monuments not just to generals but to men of letters.

Michael said, "We'll get something to eat at the railroad station."

He left me there in the big echoing restaurant, the remains of toast and scrambled eggs on my plate, while he went to the car-rental office. When he returned he said, "No record of a Colin Bracely having rented a car within the last few days, or at any other time. But he did recall renting a red English Ford sedan to a tall, dark-haired man of about thirty-five with an American accent. He looked back through his records and then told me that the man said his name was George Runceford, and had identification to prove it."

"That was Colin," I said. The maiden name of my mother and of my Aunt Evelyn, Colin's mother, had been Runce-ford. Odd, I reflected fleetingly. I knew Colin thought of himself as very bright. Probably he was, in many respects. And yet, apparently through some sort of compulsion, he had done what I had heard criminals often do, chosen as an alias one of his own family names.

"Finish your coffee," Michael said. "We'd best be on our way."

"Where—"

"Inverness, and then that private airfield."

We left the stately gray city, crossed a bridge above the River Firth, drove north through rounded hills brown

157

with heather. Before noon the clouds began to break, and by the time we reached Inverness the sun was sparkling on its River Ness. We had lunch—baked chicken pies—in a small restaurant at one end of the Ness Bridge. Customers were few, and so the sandy-haired young waitress spent most of her time beside our table, urging us to visit the museum and see the mementos of Bonnie Prince Charlie's days in Inverness. She spoke of him with such proud affection—his handsomeness, his bravery—that one might have thought he had strolled these northern streets only the previous week, instead of going to his lonely drunkard's grave in Italy more than two centuries ago.

We did not, of course, visit the museum. Instead we went to a grocery store and bought bread, cheese, liverwurst, apples, cans of orange juice, and a container of instant coffee. Then we drove out of town, past the battlefield of Culloden, where, if I recalled my high school history correctly, the toops of George the Second's fat and ugly son had soundly whipped handsome Charlie and his Highlanders. Five miles farther on we came to the small airfield in the shelter of a line of low hills.

A red-haired young man in gray coveralls emerged from the hangar, wiping greasy hands on a piece of waste. "Yes," he said in an accent so thick—a Glasgow accent, Mike later said—that I could scarcely understand him, he had been on duty the day before yesterday.

Michael asked, "Then you were here when a small plane from across the Channel landed, with a young woman passenger?"

The red-haired man smiled with reminiscent appreciation. "A blond lass."

"The man I spoke to on the phone yesterday said that

the plane flew back to France. The girl, he thought, had been picked up by a man."

"So she was."

"I don't suppose you know his name."

"No, nor what he looks like, really. He wore a tweed cap and big dark glasses that covered most of his face. But he was tall and dark-haired and about thirty-five. Both he and the girl had American accents."

Colin and Betsy, undoubtedly.

Michael asked, "What kind of car was he driving?"

"A red Ford, with rental license plates."

"Do you have any idea where they went?"

I waited, breath held, while the man in coveralls hesitated. He started to shake his head and then said, "Wait! Perhaps I do. The man asked if he could use the loo, and while he was gone the girl reached into the Ford's glove compartment and took out a map and unfolded it. I walked over to the car, thinking there might be something she'd want to ask. She said something about there being a lot of funny names in Scotland, like Lossiemouth, for instance, and I said yes, that was true. As we were both looking down at the map I noticed that someone had put a circle in blue ink around Marsaig."

Michael asked, "Marsaig?"

"It's a village quite a ways west and north of here in the Highlands. Never been there, myself. Of course, perhaps the map had nothing to do with them. Perhaps someone who had rented the car earlier had left it. Anyway, as I was about to ask her where they were going, the man came back to the car and gave me a look that said he'd like to murder me. Jealous, I suppose. Then he got in the car and drove off with the girl toward Inverness, although whether they went there or not I couldn't say."

Michael thanked him. We, too, started back toward Inverness, but we'd gone only a few hundred yards when Michael pulled over to the side of the road and stopped. He said, "Will you reach into the door pocket and hand me that road guide?"

The road guide was not a map but a paperbacked book containing many maps, each covering several square miles of territory of England, Scotland, or Ireland. I sat there, vaguely aware of some sort of birdsong—a lark's perhaps?—spilling down through the bright air while he studied the maps. Finally he said, "Here's Marsaig, over in Ross and Cromarty County, near the Sutherland border."

He put the car in gear. A few miles farther on we turned right onto a narrow road that led through rolling hills tawny with heather. Steadily the land grew more rugged, and the road narrower and more rutted. At last it was wide enough for only one vehicle, so that when we saw another motorist approaching, which happened infrequently indeed, either we or the other car had to pull into one of the frequent turnouts and wait for the other to pass. Not only the road's condition slowed our progress. Also there were sheep. Again and again great, slow-moving flocks of them barred our way, turning to look at us with black faces as the Land-Rover inched forward. Sometimes, when Michael tapped the horn, a sheep would turn and stare at us with apparent reproof for several seconds before ambling to one side of the road.

I was aware, though, that if we had been here on any other sort of errand, I would not have cared how long the journey lasted. All around us was the beauty of the Highlands, a beauty that seemed touched with melancholy, as if the land had absorbed some of the tragedy of Scottish history. Wave after wave of mountains, stripped bare of trees generations ago to make masts for English ships, changed color in the ever-changing light, sometimes brown, sometimes dark blue, sometimes purple, and, as the day neared its end, even a deep rose for a few moments now and then. And everywhere there was the sound of moving water. The gurgle of the little brooks down the mountainsides, frothing as they dropped from ledge to ledge. The louder roar of rivers in the valley, foaming around jagged black rocks. And once, when we stopped beside a loch shadowed in a deep valley so that Michael could consult the map, I heard the lap of wavelets on the pebbly shore. The sound, blending with the whisper of wind through the heather and the ringing of distant sheep bells, made a haunting music.

Daylight was fading when, on a road lonelier and rougher than any we had traversed so far, we saw a weather-bleached wooden sign: "Marsaig, 2 miles." The town, beside a roaring river, consisted of one abandoned stone building that, Michael said, probably once had been a distillery. There were also a half-dozen small stone cottages and one business establishment, a combination grocery store, bakery, and gas station. When the elderly proprietor had filled the Land-Rover's tank, Michael asked, "Did a red Ford drive through here in the last couple of days?"

Pulses racing, I watched the old man consider. Finally he said, "Seems to me a red car did go past here two days ago. Maybe it was a Ford. It didn't stop, and my eyesight isn't much good for anything more than a few yards. I'm sure, though, that there was a man and a woman in it."

We thanked him and drove away. It was growing dark

rapidly now. About a half-mile farther on Mike turned off the road and drove down a sloping bank to a loch's edge. Not knowing where the place was to which Colin had taken my sister, whether twenty miles away or around the next bend, we did not light a fire, but ate a supper of bread and cheese and one slice of liverwurst apiece. While we ate, I asked the question that had been on my mind for several hours.

"Michael, do you have a gun with you?"

"Yes."

Feeling relieved that he had it, and yet dismayed at the thought of his using it, I finished my meal in silence.

We crawled into the sleeping bag after that. I remember the river of dark sky, strewn with stars, between the ranges of mountains on either side of the narrow valley. My last recollection of that night is Michael's sleeping breath, mingled with the lap of wavelets on the shore, and, from someplace high in the darkness, the cry of a night bird.

EIGHTEEN

The first light awoke us. The water of the loch was so cold that it seemed to burn my skin when I splashed it on my face, and made my teeth ache slightly when I brushed them. Now that it was day, we thought it safe to light the primus stove. While we heated water, Michael shaved with a razor plugged into the car's dashboard. We had a breakfast of instant coffee and bread and cheese, and then, with everything stored away, drove the Land-Rover in low gear up to the road.

It was nearly two hours later—hours in which we had not seen a house, or another car, or another human being— that we rounded a bend to find a flock of sheep ahead. They were accompanied by a young boy and by two noisy little collies—Border collies, Mike had told me they were called. We inched our way through the woolly, bleating mass. Then Michael stopped the car and beckoned to the boy.

He was about twelve, with red-brown hair near the

shade of mine and many more freckles, not just across the bridge of his nose but all over his face. Mike asked, "Did you happen to see a red Ford on this stretch of road sometime during the past few days?"

He didn't hesitate, as had the old man at the gas station. "Happen I did, and a mean sod was driving it, too." Then, with a quick glance at me: "Begging your pardon, ma'am."

Mike asked, "What did he do?"

"Tried to bull his way through my sheep! Almost hit my best ewe."

"Was there anyone with him?"

The boy nodded. "A bonny young lady. Why someone like her should be with a sod like him—" Again he threw me an apologetic glance.

Mike asked, "Do you have any idea where they went?"

"Happen I do, mister." Then, as my heartbeats quickened, he went on. "A cousin of mine, Ben McNab, lives in a glen about five miles from here. Every day he drives his sheep out of the glen and a few miles down the road to pasture, and then drives them back at night. I thought the man in the Ford might have treated his flock the same way, so that night I walked to his place and asked him.

"You see," he went on, "it's against the law in Scotland for a motorist to put livestock in danger. I thought that if Ben would back me up we might give the sod what he deserves." No apologetic glance this time. "But Ben hadn't seen him at all."

Mike said slowly, "Then probably the Ford turned off someplace before he reached your cousin's flock."

The boy nodded. "Before they'd gone five miles they must have driven up one of the glens, and then driven back down to the road sometime after dark. Although why

164

somebody should go up those glens I don't know, except to shoot grouse, and he didn't look like a grouse hunter. What I mean, there's nothing up those glens *but* grouse. Oh, some old crofts, but nobody lives in them. The land's no good anymore, not even for winter pasturage, let alone farming."

"Are you sure that no one has tried to fix up one of those crofts?"

The boy frowned. "Come to think of it, I did hear about somebody—some kind of foreigner, a Frenchman or Italian, maybe—leasing a croft from whoever owns it. Some land company in Edinburgh, I guess. The fellow was going to put new thatch on the croft so he could use it as a hunting lodge, people said. But I never saw him."

"Perhaps the man in the Ford—"

The boy shook his head emphatically. "*He* was a Yank. I know because when I yelled at him he yelled back, something about why didn't I keep my effing"—again a glance at me—"sheep off the road."

We thanked him and drove on, edging our way carefully through the sheep, which, by that time, had ambled past us with their barking escorts.

To our left pebble-strewn ground, crisscrossed by tiny rivulets, sloped down to a broad, quiet river that, unless I was mistaken, drained the loch on whose shore we had slept the night before. Now and then clumps of willow grew along the river's bank. To our right rose the rugged hills, covered with bracken, and draped with wind-stirred streamers of foaming burns that plummeted from ledge to ledge, and so deeply folded that every few hundred yards or so we passed the entrance to a shadowy glen. We drove very slowly, almost coming to a stop at the glen entrances, most of them so choked with stones and bracken that no vehicle could have driven up them, at least not for many years. A few, though, displayed faint wheel marks that led upward into the shadows.

At last Michael came to a complete stop. Without speaking, he left the Land-Rover, walked back a few steps. After a moment he called, "Jenny!" and I got out and went to stand beside him.

At least one vehicle had driven up that glen recently. Two lines of crushed bracken testified to that. What was more, a small jagged boulder near the right-hand wheel mark bore a narrow streak of red. I pictured a car, squeezing past the boulder into the narrow passage. . . .

I said, in a hushed voice, "Are you sure it's car paint?"

"Of course I'm not sure. But it's certainly worth investigating."

We got back into the Land-Rover. Michael drove it off the road and over pebble-strewn earth and then stopped in the shelter of a clump of willows beside the smooth river. When he turned to me his usually calm manner held unmistakable tension.

"Think you're up to a bit of climbing?"

I nodded.

Moving swiftly, he opened the car's trunk and took out the sleeping bag. That morning he had folded it over and rolled it up, securing it with two looped straps that, at either end of the roll, could be slipped over the shoulders.

"Think you can carry this?"

Again I nodded. With its thermal lining and nylon exterior, the sleeping bag, although warm, was lightweight. He packed a rucksack with all that remained of our food, a coil of stout-looking cord, a flashlight, and the Thermos he had filled with river water. Last of all he reached under the car's dashboard for the revolver, a blunt-nosed one about eight inches long. My stomach curled. Guns have always repelled me. He stowed it in the right-hand pocket of his dark green windbreaker and buttoned the flap. He lifted the rucksack onto his back, then held the sleeping bag while I slipped my arms though the carrying straps.

"All set?"

Afraid that my nervousness would show in my voice, I nodded my answer.

We walked back over the pebbly earth, leaping across wider rivulets, and climbed to the road. On the other side of it we entered the deeply shadowed glen. We followed the wheel tracks only a few yards. Then, with Mike in the lead, we started up one steeply slanted wall of the narrow canyon and climbed through rocks and bracken and clumps of red-berried rowan trees until we had almost reached the crest. Then Michael turned to our right along the steep hillside. Without his telling me, I knew I must move as quietly as possible, trying not to break branches or dislodge pebbles.

Gradually the glen curved. Gradually, too, it widened, and its walls grew less precipitous. Looking down, I saw the remains of what once must have been a pen for sheep or cattle, its collapsed rails forming a roughly octagonal pattern in the tall, wild grass.

We worked our way around another curve. Suddenly my blood surged so strongly that I felt a tingling in my fingertips. Below us on a grassy, almost level stretch stood a stone cottage. Its roof appeared newly thatched. Smoke curled from its chimney, bluish-gray in the glen's shadows.

A few yards from the stone croft, near an old shed with

gaping holes in its thatched roof, stood two cars. One was a red sedan. The other was a dark blue sports car. I couldn't identify the make, but it looked both European and expensive.

Then, through the drumming of the blood in my ears, I became aware of another sound, The Sting's "Roll 'em Easy."

My sister in there, with transistor radio tuned loud, and perhaps dancing to that heavy beat?

Michael and I looked at each other silently. Then, with a gesture, he signaled that we were to turn around and go back.

We retreated only a few yards, stopping at a fairly level spot, a kind of ledge backed by a short stretch of solid rock. Through a clump of rowan trees, rooted below the edge, we could see back up the glen to the croft.

I said, almost in a whisper, "Braselmo's car?"

"The blue one? It must be."

"Then the doctor who is going to—going to—"

"It appears he hasn't arrived yet."

Unless, I thought, my stomach gathering into a sick knot, he had come up here with Braselmo. After all, Mike was only guessing that the doctor would want to spend as little time up here as he could, and so would arrive as late as possible, and, after it was all over, slip away quickly. It sounded logical. But there might be other considerations, ones we didn't know about, that had impelled him to accompany Braselmo up here. Perhaps, I thought, with that knot in my stomach growing even tighter, perhaps already—

Almost as if in answer to the prayer forming in my thoughts, the croft's door opened. Rock music blasted out into that isolated place. And my sister, in chinos and a pink turtleneck sweater, sauntered out onto the long grass.

The music ceased. A man I had last seen at a sidewalk café on Manhattan's Columbus Avenue appeared in the doorway. He shouted, "Do you have to leave that damned thing on even when you go outside?" and slammed the door.

My sister shrugged. She looked thinner than she had in Paris only a few days before, and very bored. But with infinite thankfulness I saw, as she walked over to the blue sports car, that she moved as gracefully as ever.

She grasped the top of the car door. Her feet, in white sneakers, assumed the First Position. Here in this remote northern glen, my sister went through the ballet exercises I had seen her perform ever since early childhood in ballet schools, and in the sun parlor of the Carrsville house, and in the living room of that Queens condominium.

As I watched her extend a right leg straight backward and dip a gracefully curved right arm toward the grass, I wondered what sort of explanation they had given her for bringing her here. That detectives hired by Braselmo's wife were hot on the trail, and that they must find some really remote hiding place? Something like that, perhaps.

Betsy stopped her exercising. She started toward the cottage, then stopped and looked around her. Her bored-looking gaze swept past the place where Michael and I watched through the rowan trees. She went into the house, closed the door. A moment later the radio started blasting again. Despite my terrible fear for her, I felt fleeting amusement at the thought of how much irritation she must be causing her middle-aged "fiancé." How he must long to smash that radio to bits. But probably he regarded the annoyance as a small price to pay to keep her reasonably content and compliant.

The day lengthened. Once more Betsy opened the door, but instead of coming out onto the grass she sat on the doorstep for a while, face resting on her balled fists, while the Rolling Stones shattered the glen's ancient silence. After ten minutes or so she went back in. About an hour later the door again opened. With a tightening of my nerves I saw that the man who came out was Colin. He walked to the Ford and reached inside for something. Probably it was a fresh pack of cigarettes, because a moment later, standing beside the car, he put a cigarette in his mouth and lighted it. The warm color of the match flame made me realize how much the light had faded.

Colin went back inside. Michael and I sat there, knees drawn up, shoulders touching, talking now and then in low voices, while the shadows thickened, merged into a solid darkness broken only by the glow of lamplight through the croft's window. We had our supper, a frugal one of bread and about a third of the remaining cheese and liverwurst, washed down with cold water from the Thermos. Even if we had brought the primus stove up there with us, we wouldn't have dared use it.

I wondered how long our food would hold out. Surely long enough. My cousin and Braselmo must have tried to make certain that their stay up here would be as brief as possible. And that, of course, would require that the doctor join them before long.

The doctor. And, after an interval, the film of Betsy they would make. (The camera and the lights they would use. Were they in the trunk of the blue car? Stowed away somewhere in the croft?)

That old man in Switzerland. With the film as proof that his granddaughter lived, his lame granddaughter with a green fleck in one of her blue eyes, he would gladly hand over the money. And by that time Betsy would be— where? Someplace in this glen, with bracken and stones strewn over the disturbed earth to conceal it?

I must not think about that. If I did, I would not sleep. And it might be important indeed that I get sufficient sleep.

It was eight-fifteen by the luminous dial of my wrist-watch when we unrolled the sleeping bag. Fully clothed, we slid between the layers of thermal wool. In spite of the nervous and physical strain of that long day I had feared I would stay awake, but, with my head on Mike's shoulder, I went to sleep almost immediately.

NINETEEN

Again the first gray light awoke me. Michael had managed to slip out of the sleeping bag without disturbing me. Now he stood motionless a few feet away, looking down into the glen.

I joined him. Darkness in the little valley was still so thick that the croft was only a pale, indistinct shape, with no smoke curling from its chimney.

Mike said, in a low voice, "I've been thinking. If he's coming today, he'll arrive fairly early." I knew that he meant the doctor. "He won't want to risk driving up the glen once the light begins to fade."

"And so what should we—"

"We'd better go back to the glen's entrance. That way we can stop him before there's any chance of those two down there hearing the sound of his engine."

We placed the rolled-up sleeping bag and the knapsack behind a clump of furze. When Michael slung the coil of stout cord over one shoulder I forbore to ask him why.

Moving as quietly as possible through the cool gray light, we retraced our steps of the afternoon before. We stopped finally in a grove of rowans only a few feet above the wheel tracks and perhaps thirty yards from the glen's mouth. From there the road was plainly visible. We sat down, backs resting against slender tree trunks.

By then the sun was up, although now and again a patch of drifting fog obscured its light. By ten the fog had disappeared, and strange as it seemed that far north in the month of October, we began to feel comfortably warm in that sheltered spot.

Twice, flocks of bleating sheep passed along the road. Neither time were they accompanied by a shepherd or by collies. Evidently they had just taken it into their stubborn heads to go for a mass stroll. Twice, too, we grew tense at the sound of an approaching car. But once the vehicle was a battered truck with an elderly Scot, incongruously clad in denim overalls and a plaid tam-o'-shanter, at the wheel. The second time the car was a Volvo station wagon. A man drove, with a woman curled up in a far corner of the seat, apparently asleep. Two small girls peered out the rear window.

The sound of the Volvo's engine died away. Silence after that except for the whisper of wind, and now and then the ringing of distant sheep bells, and, constantly, the faint rippling of that shallow river across the road. It was a sound that kept me reminded of a growing thirst. I longed to run across the road, kneel on the pebbly riverbank, and scoop up water in my two hands. But I must not. If I did, ill luck might decree that the man we awaited would come along just then and, seeing me near the glen's entrance, take fright and drive on.

By tacit agreement we said little. I think both of us were apprehensive that we might hear the sound of one or both of those men back there coming down the glen, either on foot or by car.

Instead, shortly before two o'clock, we heard a vehicle approaching very slowly along the road. It drove past the glen's mouth, an old gray Morris with a badly dented right-hand front door. A moment later the sound of the engine ceased. A car door creaked open. Then the driver reappeared, on foot, at the glen opening.

He halted. He was a fat man in a cheap-looking gray business suit that appeared strange indeed in this wild place. His eyes, searching the steep slope opposite the one where we sat hidden, apparently saw something that Michael and I had missed—a bit of colored cloth tied to a furze bush, perhaps. Anyway, it must have convinced him that he had reached the right place, because he turned and walked back toward where he had left his car. Through the pounding of blood in my ears I heard the car door slam, heard the engine start up.

Mike was on his feet now. I saw him unzip his windbreaker pocket and take out that little gun. Dimly aware that my legs felt weak, I, too, stood up.

The old car reappeared, backing past the glen's entrance. Then the driver, shifting gears, turned sharply onto the narrow track.

Mike plunged down the slope and, gun raised, stood in the car's path. Fear made my heart contract. Could Michael leap out of the way in time if that man, ignoring the gun pointed at the windshield, drove straight ahead? But he did not. Instead he came to an abrupt stop. Either he switched off the ignition or the engine stalled, because its throbbing ceased. Mike said softly, "Get out with your hands up. And don't make any noise. Don't even close the car door."

The man obeyed, swinging the door open. I heard his panting breath as, with hands raised, he slowly, laboriously squirmed his way under the steering wheel. He stood before us, hands still raised, a gray-skinned man of fifty-odd in a cheap-looking gray suit and a gray felt hat.

He was very fat. Of about average height, he must have weighed close to three hundred pounds. And it was not solid-looking fat. I had the impression that under the shiny suit of some synthetic material, under the wrinkled white shirt, his flesh hung in loose folds.

Mike said, "What's your name?"

Fear in the prominent brown eyes with the bruised-looking circles beneath them. "Slocum. Harold Slocum."

"*Dr.* Slocum?"

"Yes."

There had been more than fear in that one syllable. There had been so much guilt and self-loathing that, under other circumstances, I might have felt sorry for him.

Mike called in a soft voice, "Jenny!"

On shaking legs I made my way down the slope to stand beside him. He said, "Find out if that really is his name. Look at the registration slip inside the car."

I looked. The car was registered to Harold Slocum, M.D., of 39 Bryselin Street, London. And on the passenger's side of the front seat was further proof of who he was, a doctor's instrument bag. Probably it had been of inferior leather to start with, and now it was badly scuffed, as well as splitting along one seam. Flaking gold letters on one side said, "Harold Slocum, M.D." I forced myself to grasp the handles, hold up the bag for Mike to see. "That's his name, all right," I said, and dropped the bag back onto the seat.

Mike waved the gun. "All right, Dr. Slocum."

The fat man climbed ahead of us up to the clump of trees. At Mike's orders, he laboriously lowered himself to the ground and then lay on his side, hands behind his back. While I held the gun, Mike wound cord around his wrists and ankles. Then he dragged the bound man to a sitting position, his back against a tree trunk.

Mike took the gun from my hand and restored it to his windbreaker pocket. "All right, Dr. Slocum. Why did you come here?"

The man was weeping now, head lowered, triple chins pressing against his chest. "You must know," he said. "Otherwise you wouldn't have interfered with me."

"Yes, we know, but we want to hear it from you."

"There's this young girl," he said, after several moments. Because of his weeping and his lowered head, it was hard to understand him. "They wanted me to operate on her foot, so that it would look as if she'd been born with—a club foot."

"Who's 'they'?"

"They told me they were Maurice Silvano and George Chandler, but I don't think those are their real names."

"Why did they want you to operate?"

"So they could palm her off as—someone else. After her foot healed enough they were going to make—make a film of her."

"Walking?"

"Yes. And—and close-ups of her foot. Then they'd show it to him—"

"Him?"

"They never told me his name. They just said he'd pay them a lot of money."

"How much were they going to pay you?"

"A hundred thousand pounds." He was sobbing now. "I didn't want to do it. Do you think anyone would, except some kind of monster? And I'm not that. It's just that all my life . . ."

Like the tears, words were gushing from him now, self-justifying words that he himself must have known were inadequate. Even though Mike, like me, must have been afraid that those two back at the stone croft might appear at any moment, he let the man talk. I'm not sure why. Maybe he hoped to gain some information that would be of value to us. Maybe the fat man aroused in him, as he did in me, not only disgust but a reluctant compassion. Anyway, Mike let him talk.

Harold Slocum was fifty-nine. He'd been born poor, the son of a merchant seaman who had disappeared when the boy was three, and he'd been born with a tendency to put on fat. "As long as I can remember, people either laughed at the sight of me, or looked repelled."

All through his teenage years he had worked after school and during holidays and saved his money to go to medical school. "I thought my life would be all right once I was a doctor, but it wasn't. People don't like being treated by a man who looks like me. And I've never been able to lose weight, at least not for long."

Nevertheless, he had managed to win a wife, a girl he'd met when he bought a ticket from her at a cinema box office. "I guess she thought marrying a doctor would be a step up in the world. When she saw I'd probably never make much more than a bare living, she walked out and got a divorce."

The institution of socialized medicine hadn't helped him much. "Even with the state paying for their treatment, patients get to choose among the doctors registered for the program, and not many chose me.

"Then a few weeks ago this man with a foreign accent, a good-looking chap in his forties, struck up a conversation with me in a pub." Slocum had been pleased. He'd never had many friends. They had dinner together several times. Then, in a roundabout way, his new friend had made the proposition.

"I was horrified at first. But he pointed out that the girl would be gaining as well as losing. Once this man was convinced she was who he wanted her to be, she'd be rich for the rest of her life."

Mike's voice was harsh. "You believed that? You believed that they'd let her live? You must have known that once they had that film and could collect the money—"

"I wanted to believe! And I felt *I* ought to get something out of life. You see, there's this woman, not some calculating young tart, but a nice woman about ten years younger than myself. She's my landlady. I think that if I could tell her I'd inherited a nice bit of money, she'd marry me. We could leave England and spend the rest of our lives in some warm place where the living is cheap, and where, if I wanted to practice, there wouldn't be much competition—"

Several minutes before, he had stopped crying, but now the tears were flowing again. "You're right. I didn't really think they'd let her—And that's why I think that once I got there I would have refused to do it, after all."

179

Chin sunk on his chest, he fell silent except for his quiet weeping. Mike took the gun from his pocket, handed it to me. "Wait here."

"Where are you—"

"I'm going to drive his car across the road and park it beside the Land-Rover in among those willows. We don't want to go on taking a chance that one or both of those two back there might decide to jog down to the road and back."

He knelt beside the man, unknotted his frayed red-and-white polka-dotted tie, and removed it from the fat neck. "Open your mouth." Mike put the gag in place and tied it behind the fat man's head.

He said, getting to his feet, "Keep an eye on him, although I don't see how he can give you any trouble. Would you like me to bring you back some water? We should have brought the Thermos with us, but I think there's an old canvas canteen in the Land-Rover."

"Oh, yes, please. I'm thirsty."

Mike descended to the old Morris sedan, backed it onto the road. I could still hear the growl of its engine as he drove it in low gear across the pebbled flats to the river. The fat man, gaze lowered, remained motionless. I stared at him, held by a loathing fascination touched with pity. When it came right down to it, would he actually have reneged on his promise to Braselmo and Colin? I doubted it. After all, if he had, they never would have let him go free, perhaps to report to the police. Still, at the last moment he might have found himself unable to keep the bargain—

The faint swish of footsteps through bracken. I turned to see Michael climbing the slope. He carried a coil of

180

rope over his shoulder, a dripping canteen in his left hand, and in his right a four-sided metal can. I knew it contained kerosene because I had seen him pour fuel from it onto the little primus stove.

He set down the kerosene tin, took the gun from my hand and restored it to his pocket, unstoppered the canteen, and handed it to me. I drank deeply. Mike drank after that, and then said to Slocum, "I'll untie that gag for a moment if you want a drink of water."

The fat man shook his head.

With the coil of rope Mike bound him securely to the tree trunk, passing the rope around his body several times. Then we left him there and started back up the glen, Mike carrying the canteen and the kerosene tin.

I didn't ask why he had brought kerosene. I was almost sure I knew.

TWENTY

At three in the afternoon the depths of the narrow glen were sunless and the air was rapidly cooling. As on the day before, we moved cautiously, but probably there was little need for our keeping quiet. When we were still fifty yards or more away from where we had left our gear, we could hear Betsy's transistor radio. By the time we reached that flat ledge overlooking the croft, though, the sound had ceased. Perhaps, although it seemed improbable, she had grown tired of the sound. More likely, it was Braselmo who had snapped Michael Jackson off in midnote.

Mike and I sat down side by side, arms wrapped around updrawn knees. Looking down through the screen of rowan leaves, I saw the croft door open. My heartbeats quickened as Betsy came out onto the tall wild grass. As on the previous afternoon, she sauntered over to the blue sports car, grasped the upper edge of its door, and went through the exercises that I, beaming with big sisterly pride, had first watched her perform as a four-year-old pupil at Miss Gloria Rose's Dance Academy.

After a while she walked a few feet from the car and sat down, cross-legged. She plucked a blade of grass, slit it with her thumbnail, blew through the slit. If she produced a whistling sound I could not hear it, not from that distance. But she was not too far away for me to sense her boredom.

And I sensed something under the boredom. Anxiety? Perhaps. The Lord knew Betsy was no intellectual. But she wasn't stupid, either. During these few days in this isolated place, surely she must have felt an occasional doubt of Braselmo's motives in having her brought here.

Or perhaps she hadn't allowed herself doubts. She wanted so desperately to replace the dream that had died along with that miserable production of *Oklahoma!*, wanted so much to believe that soon she would be a rich man's pampered wife—

She got up and went into the croft.

I said, "Michael?"

"Yes."

"I'm not sure what you intend to do. But wouldn't it be better to drive back to that tiny little town, Marsaig, and phone the nearest police barracks from there? There was a phone in that filling station. I saw it."

Michael shook his head. "I thought it through, Jenny. Of course, we could just have left that fat creep trussed up there earlier today and driven back to Marsaig and called the police. The nearest ones are at Dingwall, probably. That's the county seat.

"But what if in the meantime Braselmo and your cousin had gotten the wind up? They well might have, you know.

184

After all, they must have expected Slocum to arrive some time ago. What if, while we were driving back over those miserable, sheep-clogged roads, and then trying to persuade the police over the phone that we weren't a couple of lunatics, or druggies . . . what if, during that time, Braselmo and Colin decided that Slocum had crossed them up, and that they'd better get your sister out of here fast? Or perhaps," he added, his voice heavy with his reluctance to say the words, "they might have decided it would be safer not to bother with Betsy."

I felt an icy sensation in the pit of my stomach. Michael said, "You see? And it could still happen like that, if we leave here now. By the time we got back with the police, they might well have—have taken care of your sister, and then cleared out."

I whispered, "I see. But then how—"

"They must be armed, but I'm sure their guns are in the croft, not in their cars. If I trick them into coming out, let's hope without their guns—"

"Trick them? How? The shed?"

"Yes."

I said swiftly, "But even if they're not armed when they come out, there'll still be two of them, and only one of you. What if one of them manages to get back inside and pick up—"

"Easy! Take it easy." His arm went around my shoulders. "I'll have you on my side."

"What is it you want me to—"

"There's a locked room, or maybe just a closet or cupboard, in that house. I figure there has to be. I'll want you to find it for me."

He paused and then added, "But there's no use in

185

looking too far ahead. When the time comes, just do as I ask."

The day was fading rapidly now. Although the strip of sky above the glen, set with a ghostly first-quarter moon, was still pale, in the depths of the canyon night already had fallen. Lamplight bloomed in the croft windows.

The sky darkened. That pale quarter-moon brightened. The radio down in the stone croft, which had been playing again, fell silent. Probably they were preparing supper. Who, I wondered, was the cook? Betsy? If so, she was performing the task with neither pleasure nor skill. My sister's favorite form of meal preparation had always been phoning for Chinese takeout.

I saw Mike consult his watch. I looked at the luminous dial of my own. Six-thirty. As Mike stood up, I felt I could read his mind. Probably they would be at table now, and therefore a little off guard . . .

I got to my feet. Mike bent, lifted the can of kerosene. I heard the faint sound of a pocket zipper, saw his right hand take out the dully gleaming revolver.

His low voice said, "Follow me halfway down the slope, and then stop. Don't come any farther until I call to you. Is that clear?"

"Yes."

"And if they do come out firing, and you see me go down, don't try to help me."

I whispered, "Oh, Mike! Don't ask me to—"

"Jenny, you *couldn't* help me, not against two armed men. The only thing you would be able to do for me and for your sister would be to get to the Land-Rover as fast as possible and drive back to Marsaig and phone the police." He set down the kerosene can, plunged his hand into his trouser pocket. "Here are the car keys."

My numb fingers closed around them, then thrust them into the pocket of my chinos. He said, "Will you promise to do that? Promise not to lose your head and come running down there?"

After a moment I said, "I promise."

He bent and kissed me on the mouth, a brief, hard kiss. Then, carrying the kerosene tin, he turned and went down the slope. I followed for perhaps fifteen seconds, trying to make sure that I did not stumble over a tree trunk or lose my footing on the slippery bracken. Then he called to me softly, "Stop there."

I halted. There was just enough light for me to make out his dark shape as he moved down through the remaining trees and then across the long grass. As he approached the old shed his figure seemed to merge with its dark bulk, so that I could no longer see him.

I waited, aware of my heart's thudding. I strained to hear, through the pounding of my blood, some other sound, like the slosh of kerosene from its container, but I could not.

Then I saw him coming toward me. He moved slowly, bent over. I saw a faint gleam, and realized he was laying a kerosene trail across the grass.

He straightened, walked a step or two, set down the can. I saw him turn, crouch down. A match flared. Then a line of fire raced over the grass, leaped onto the kerosene-soaked shed. Dimly I was aware that Mike had retreated to the first line of trees at the foot of the slope.

Already the shed blazed furiously. Sparks flew skyward. Interspersed with the crackle of flames were the explosive popping sounds of dry old timber.

The croft's door burst open and two men ran out, their faces recognizable even at that distance in the fire's glow. My cousin stopped short, staring at the blaze. Shouting obscenities, Braselmo raced toward that expensive sports car parked perilously close to the blazing shed. Dimly I was aware of my sister, standing in the croft's doorway, her face bewildered-looking in the dancing light of the flames.

I became aware, too, that Michael had moved farther onto the grass. He shouted, "Braselmo! Stop right where you are, both of you, or I'll shoot."

The older man did halt, as if suddenly frozen, but my cousin whirled, darted toward the croft's doorway.

Mike fired.

I saw Colin stagger, saw his left hand go to his right shoulder. Running forward, Mike shouted, "Stand facing the house wall, both of you."

They obeyed, Braselmo with alacrity, Colin a little unsteadily, his hand still clutching his shoulder. Mike hurried through the reddish, wavering light to stand a few feet behind them. "Jenny!"

I ran the rest of the way down the slope. It was not until I reached the grass that I realized Betsy was outside the house now and screaming at Mike, "Who are you? What are you *doing*?"

"Betsy!"

She whirled to look in my direction. "Jenny?" Bewilderment and terror in her voice, she said, "Is that you, Jenny?"

"Be quiet, Betsy!"

Instead, even though I was close to her now, she cried, even more loudly, "That man shot Colin! What's happening? What are you *doing* here? You promised you wouldn't interfere." She was screaming now. "You promised!"

I slapped her. She stood rigid for a moment, and then began to whimper.

I said, "Those men were going to kill you."

"Jenny," Mike called, "find out about that locked room."

Betsy had found her voice again. "You've gone crazy. How can you say that they were going to—Why, Tony and I are going to be—"

"All right, so I'm crazy. But there's a locked room somewhere in that cottage. Where is it, and where's the key?"

"Locked room! There are no locks, just the thumblatch inside my room. That just shows how crazy—" She broke off and then said, after a long, long moment, "There's the cellar. It's padlocked. I've never been down there."

There had been a shaken note in her voice. It told me that she was beginning to believe what I had said. "Where is the key to the padlock?"

Those beautiful blue eyes, stunned-looking now, moved to the two men who, with that revolver at their backs, sullenly faced the croft's stone wall. She said, still in that hushed voice, "Tony keeps it in his right jacket pocket, I think."

Through that wavering, ruddy light I moved toward the men. Braselmo did not turn his head, but his gaze, as coldly malevolent as a snake's, slid toward me. Fighting down repulsion, I dipped my hand quickly into the pocket of his natty suede jacket, found the key on its ring, stepped back.

189

My cousin had not looked at me. His hand no longer clutched his wound, and so I could see the spreading red stain on the shoulder of his white cable-knit sweater. I turned and, aware that Betsy moved with me, hurried into the croft.

I gained a swift impression of a fairly large room, bathed in the glow of an oil lamp that stood on a dish-cluttered table. Opposite the croft's entrance a partly open door gave me a glimpse of a narrow bed and, hanging from a hook, Besty's old red raincoat. On one side of the room wooden stairs led up to the loft. The men, I reflected fleetingly, must have been bedding down up there.

But most of my attention was centered on that cellar door in the middle of the room. Flush with the floor, it was secured by a padlock-fastened hasp. An iron ring recessed in the center of the door provided the means of raising it.

I knelt, unlocked the padlock, laid it aside. I stood up, placed the key on the dining table, and then said to my sister, "Help me."

Each of us grasping the ring in a right hand, we managed to raise the door until it stood upright on its hinges. I lifted the lamp from the table. Aware that Betsy followed, I descended rough wooden steps.

Although dirt-floored, the cellar appeared meticulously clean. In one corner stood a table holding a movie camera, small and light enough to be held in the hand. Hung from the wall above it were several large acetylene lanterns. They must have planned to use them, I thought, feeling sick, to provide sufficient light for the film.

At the far end of the cellar, an even more powerful-looking lantern hung above a narrow table. Metal-legged, its surface covered with some sort of plastic sheeting, it stood about three and a half feet high. A shelf on the wall near it held tall bottles, a metal tray, a roll of something— sterile cotton, I supposed—wrapped in blue paper, and other objects my sick gaze could not identify.

Betsy said, almost in a whisper, "That table over there. It looks like . . ." Her voice trailed off.

No time now to think of ways to tell her as gently as possible. "It is. They were going to have someone operate on your foot."

The color drained from her face, leaving it green-white. "Operate?"

"Later on, when your foot was more or less healed, they'd have made movies of you to send to a rich old man in Switzerland."

Although she made no sound, her lips framed the word "Why?"

"Because he'd agreed to pay them lots of money for proof that his granddaughter was alive. She was kidnapped fifteen years ago, when she was four." I paused, and then said with a rush, "She was blond and blue-eyed, with a green fleck in her right eye. She also had been born with a clubfoot."

Betsy swayed. I reached out and grasped her arms. "Betsy! You mustn't faint. We have to help Mike. Now get back upstairs."

Carrying the lamp, I followed her up. When she reached the croft's main room she collapsed, shaking all over, onto a chair that someone had shoved back from the table. I put the lamp down near her and hurried outside to tell Mike the cellar door was open.

I came back in and stood holding the lamp beside the

opening in the floor while the two men, at Mike's order, descended the rough stairs. Apparently Colin's wound no longer bled; the red stain on his shoulder appeared to be drying. Well, I thought grimly, they wouldn't have to remain in darkness down there. Colin was a smoker. They could light one of those lanterns. They could even treat Colin's wound. Surely one of the bottles on that shelf held an antiseptic.

Michael let the heavy door fall, threaded the padlock through the hasp, snapped it shut. Straightening, he turned to my sister. "I'm Mike Baker."

She just stared at him, her blue eyes enormous.

He turned to me. "Think you two girls can walk out of the glen and drive back to Marsaig?"

"Oh, Mike! Can't you come with—"

"I'd better not. I don't suppose there's more than one chance in a hundred that those two can get out, but as long as there's any chance at all I'll stay here. When you get to Marsaig, call the police in Dingwall." He paused and then added, "Use the flashlight, of course. I placed it up there beside the rucksack."

I put my hand under Betsy's elbow, drew her to her feet. She came with me docilely enough. Outside I saw that the fire had burned itself down to a patch of embers still glowing in the grass. Braselmo's sports car, I noticed, apparently had suffered no damage.

We crossed to the steep hillside, climbed to the little ledge where Mike and I had slept the night before. After I had picked up the flashlight I hesitated. Should we try to make our way along the hillside? No, there was no reason why we shouldn't take the easier route along the glen's floor.

192

That first-quarter moon was still up. By its glow and that of the flashlight we moved quite easily between the wheel tracks. Betsy, following me, made a whimpering sound now and then, but she didn't speak.

When we were only a few yards from the glen's mouth I stopped. I couldn't just walk past him—

I turned, climbed the hillside to the grove of rowans. The fat man bound to the tree trunk blinked in the flashlight's glare.

No need now for that gag. I laid the flashlight on the ground. Overcoming my reluctance to touch him, I unknotted the necktie, dropped it beside him.

Straightening, I asked, "Are you cold?"

"A little." Then I realized, from the way his gaze shifted, that Betsy had climbed the slope to stand beside me. I also saw from the pain and guilt in his face that he had realized who she must be.

"Is there a blanket in the car?"

He nodded. "In the back seat."

"I'll bring it to you."

I turned away and, with Betsy following, descended the slope. We had almost reached the road when she spoke for the first time since we had left the croft. "Was he— was he the one who was going to—"

"Yes," I said.

That seemed to release something inside her. She wept stormily as I led her across the road, across the rivulet-laced flats to the willow grove. I unlocked the Land-Rover's door and Betsy, still weeping, got inside. The rear door of the old Morris was unlocked. I reached inside and with the same sense of distaste I had felt when I unknotted his necktie, drew out a lap robe of faded plaid.

Moments later, as I spread the robe over him, the fat man didn't look at me, just moved his lips in a soundless "Thank you." Through the thin moonlight I went back to the Land-Rover, got into the front seat beside my still-crying sister, and, after driving across the pebbly flat, headed down that narrow road toward Marsaig.

TWENTY-ONE

The month was July, and so the restaurant near the departure lounge at Heathrow was filled with young men and women who, the previous week, had appeared with varying success on the courts at Wimbledon. Not that I could see anyone really famous. No Navratilova or Lendl. Still, it was the tennis players, their arms loaded with canvas-sheathed rackets, who were getting all the attention, not Mike and Betsy and I, seated with Betsy's boyfriend at a corner table.

A few months earlier, it would have been very different. During that long trial Betsy and I could scarcely venture outside our Dingwall hotel room without flashbulbs going off in our faces. But I guess nothing or no one commands public attention for very long. Within a week after the jury's verdict, a British cabinet member had been caught in flagrante delicto with the wife of a Soviet diplomat, and then the photographers were hounding them, not the Carr sisters and Mike Baker.

The trial had been long, mainly because the death of one of the jurors had caused a lengthy delay, but the outcome had never been in doubt. Colin and Braselmo's lawyers had kept them off the stand, but Harold Slocum had testified freely. So had Armand Perrault, who, despite his years, had come to Dingwall, enraged and bitterly disappointed, from that luxurious eyrie in Switzerland.

Still another witness had been the young man with the lank, blondish hair and a faint scar on his upper lip who had rung the bell of Colin's flat that September evening and then stood scowling in the hall while I looked at him through the mirrored peephole. It was he who, on Colin's instruction, had followed me back to Ebury Street my first night in London. Two days later, in the farther reaches of Kew Gardens, he had fired a rifle at Mike and me, not to hurt us but to just give us "a good scare, so that the newspaper bloke would lay off and the girl go back to the States." He had never been able to collect, though, the full amount Colin had promised him, even though he'd gone to Colin's Soho flat several times. Frustrated, he had decided to "collect" by testifying against Colin and Braselmo.

When the case finally reached the jury, its verdict was swift. Both men were found guilty of conspiracy to commit murder and sentenced to ten years' imprisonment.

Accompanied by both my sister and Mike, I was to fly back across the Atlantic now. In Queens we would put the condominium in the hands of a broker. In Carrsville we would do the same with that Victorian house.

And, not at all incidentally, Mike and I would get married.

We had postponed marriage until now because we had feared the press would make a field day of the occasion.

196

Besides, I liked the idea of getting married in that old house before it passed forever out of the hands of the Carr family.

Across the table from us Betsy's boyfriend, who had come to Heathrow to see us off, said something that made her giggle. I thought of the contrast between this ebullient girl and the one who, that October night, had wept hysterically beside me as I drove to Marsaig.

But I think that once we had reached the tiny settlement, and once we had aroused the owner of the gas station–grocery store, it was Betsy who had ensured the swift arrival of the Dingwall police. While I was trying to explain the situation, she snatched the phone from my hand and screamed into it, "You just come here right now! *Then* you can ask questions."

With eighteen-year-old resilience, Betsy returned almost to normal within a few days after cell doors in the Dingwall jail slammed behind Colin and Braselmo. And the weeks of publicity during the trial brought her certain compensation. Oh, not that the Royal Ballet invited her into its ranks. But she did do some TV commercials. And she met a young BBC executive, the obviously adoring young man who sat beside her now. And she had been promised a small role in a British soap opera.

The loudspeaker called our flight. I thought, the next time I see this place, I'll be Mike's wife. And until we find a house we like, I'll live with him in that flat with the locomotive prints, and the view of the canal, and the ducks . . .

My thought must have communicated itself to Mike, because he smiled down at me and clasped my hand, and held it all the way to the gate.